TIL DEATH

Aryanna

Lock Down Publications and Ca$h
Presents

Til Death

A Novel by *Aryanna*

Lock Down Publications
Po Box 944
Stockbridge, Ga 30281

Visit our website @
www.lockdownpublications.com

Lock Down Publications
Like our page on Facebook: Lock Down Publications @
www.facebook.com/lockdownpublications.ldp
Book interior design by: **Shawn Walker**
Edited by: **Kiera Northington**

Stay Connected with Us!

Text **LOCKDOWN** to 22828 to stay up-to-date with new
releases, sneak peaks, contests and more…
Thank you.

Submission Guideline.

Submit the first three chapters of your completed manuscript to ldpsubmissions@gmail.com, subject line: Your book's title. The manuscript must be in a .doc file and sent as an attachment. Document should be in Times New Roman, double spaced and in size 12 font. Also, provide your synopsis and full contact information. If sending multiple submissions, they must each be in a separate email.

Have a story but no way to send it electronically? You can still submit to LDP/Ca$h Presents. Send in the first three chapters, written or typed, of your completed manuscript to:

LDP: Submissions Dept
Po Box 944
Stockbridge, Ga 30281

DO NOT send original manuscript. Must be a duplicate.

Provide your synopsis and a cover letter containing your full contact information.

Thanks for considering LDP and Ca$h Presents.

Dedication:

This book is dedicated to the younger me in hopes that I'll never lose sight of the dreams I'm still chasing.

Acknowledgements:

So much changes on a daily basis, but God remains constant and I'm eternally grateful for that. I thank everyone who contributed to this finished product, and I thank my fans for waiting. My apologies for going M.I.A. but rest assured that I'm never far away.

I have to thank the newest influences to my growth. I wish I could say your name out loud, but we KNOW why that wouldn't be proper. You're the core of my team, and I couldn't have grown in this way without you. I thank my LOCK DOWN PUBLICATIONS fam for always being in my corner! These are movies in the making, and I know you see my vision.

Shout out to my real ones behind the g-wall, especially HONEY. Who would Dollar be without you??? Yo Duke, it's all about the LEGACY, my nigga! Stay tuned for the next move!!!

Aryanna

Chapter 1
December 2027

The sounds of the visiting room around us didn't distract me from my silent observation of my wife in front of me, nor did it eliminate all the emotions I was feeling. Even though she was the prisoner, and I was just visiting, I still understood that prison wasn't the place to display a lot of emotions. It was hard to give her words of hope when all I really wanted to give her was her freedom and the love that came with it. For the moment though, I knew she needed me to be the Gangsta ass nigga she fell in love with, which meant I had to hold it down and keep it together for the both of us. There was only one Leroy Bly in the world, and I would always be me.

"Do you trust me? Virginia, I *said* do you trust me?" I asked angrily.

"Yes Baby, I trust you with my life."

"Then know that I'm coming for you soon." I vowed, staring deeply into her blue eyes.

I stared past her, tears welling up around the love I knew she felt, and I honed in on the fear. The fear was what I was speaking to, because I knew it was what kept her up at night, and it was what wouldn't let her rest during the day. The fear of dying in her current situation was paralyzing her, and I refused to let that happen.

"Bly, I told you that your time is up."

I glared hatefully at the female Correctional Officer standing the required 6 feet away from us, and she quickly raised her hands to point at her watch.

"It's ok Leroy, I'm ok, I promise."

Her voice didn't tremble, nor did it break, despite the silent tears sliding down her soft, pale cheeks. She was a muthafuckin soldier, and she'd been in this army too long now to be broken. *that* was what I needed her to remember!

"I'm coming for you," I whispered, before gently kissing the tears away from her face.

She smiled brightly, and I saw the Blue Flameinstantly relight in her eyes. It was this part of her beauty that took my breath away. I let my hands drop from her face, and we both stood up. My 5 '10, 300lbs muscular frame always dwarfed her 5' 2, 169lb body of thick curves, but she was still my equal in all ways. She was my balance as well. Her easy smile and quick laugh were the calm my soul needed, while the spicy Italian and Irish in her were the fire I borrowed to keep pushing thru the cold. She was my Queen, my everything that mattered in this world, and that was why I refused to let the VA DOC take her from me. To lose her was to lose myself, and I'd done that once already this lifetime. Fuck a second time.

"I'll call you tonight," she promised, standing on her tiptoes while pulling on my dreadlocks so I'd bow to her.

The instant our tongues met the entire visitation room melted away, and it was just us two lost at sea. I tasted life and death on her lips while our tongues battled like only God and the Devil could. Every flame in me was lit, and I was really willing and able to destroy whole worlds by fire. I never had to ask her if she felt what I did in moments like this because I know her too well. I knew how wet her pussy was getting with each passing second, and that the temperature of her wetness was hot enough to melt glass. My swift and sudden grabbing of both of her ass cheeks and lifting her into my arms caused her to sigh, and giggle with girlish temptation before she finally pulled back.

"I told you that you're *not* making us lose these visits. They mean too much to us baby, now put me down."

"Say it like you mean it, I taunted."

"Put me down you big pussy."

This made both of us laugh as I reluctantly lowered her to the floor. I could tell by the way she looked back up at me that she'd felt the bulge of my hard dick across her stomach and chest on the way down. I laughed because I knew her fucking panties were ruined. She turned around, and looked back over her shoulder, thru her unruly blond curls, up into my dark brown eyes. When she smiled, I gave her what she wanted, and I smacked her hard across her big ole ass. Her soft moan made my dick ache and my skin tingle, almost causing me to chase her as she sauntered away. I knew that I had to let her go, though, but our time was coming. It was coming faster than a money train.

As I slip my mask up over my mouth and nose, my eyes locked with the Correctional Officer who had been impatiently waiting to end our visit for the last hour and a half. The ice in her blue-eyed stare was immediately defrosted by the threat of painful death that I intentionally projected, and she quickly turned and followed behind Gini. I kept my temper in check while exiting the visitation room and making my way out of the prison altogether. By the time I got to the passenger side of my 2028 white drop-top Camaro, my mind was back moving with the efficiency of a cooling system at a nuclear power plant.

"How did it go?" my sister Byrd asked, around a yawn as she sat up in the driver's seat.

"Too fast as always."

Once I was in the seat, she started the car and pulled off slowly through the parking lot. My eyes scanned everything from parked cars and license plates to the number of guard towers and their location. I quietly took it all in for a moment, the same way I'd done twice a month, every month, for the last 5 years. "We're good, " I stated. Without verbally responding, Byrd acknowledged my statement by driving faster away from the prison.

Even though I couldn't see her, my eyes stayed fixed on my side mirror because I knew my wife could feel me yearning to be with her. Our love was beyond words, but if I had to choose any, they would've been fitting of a science fiction movie because this shit could consume *worlds*. Only those close to us knew that, but the world would soon see.

"So, what's the move bruh? Are you ready?"

Her question caused one single solitary tear to slide down my cheek, but I smiled because I could still hear Gini calling me a *big pussy*. Only for her would I ever be soft.

"Yeah, I'm ready. We move in a week," I replied.

"God created the world in a week, and got some rest," she said, snickering. "Yeah, he did. Now I'm about to destroy it."

Chapter 2
June 2022

"Welcome Home L!"

The smile on my face was wide as I raised my glass of champagne high in the air, accepting the toast my friends and family had given. Sipping the chilled liquid gold gave me a mental vision of one who finally tasted freedom, and it tasted damn good going down.

"Welcome Home baby boy," my mom said, stepping forward out of the crowd to hug me.

"Thanks mama."

"It took your ass long enough negro," Aniyah said, punching me softly in the side.

"Shut up thing 2! You lucky that you're my sister or I'd kick your butt!"

"You ain't kickin shit Leroy, so shut up," Danielle stated.

I hadn't known that she was gonna be here, but my head immediately swung in her direction at the sound of her voice. She came from just beyond the crowd, and my mom stepped back so that she could step forward.

"Surprise to see me, huh?" Danielle asked, hugging me fiercely.

My mind flashed back to a similar reunion almost exactly 20 years prior when I'd come home from a bid in juvenile prison, and this same girl had been there to greet me. The biggest difference between now and then was that she wasn't toting around a 4-day old baby, and I wasn't about to let her suck my dick in the apartment building stairway.

"I definitely wasn't expecting to see you slim, but it's a pleasant surprise," I replied.

"I've got a better surprise for you if you want it," she whispered in my ear, before kissing my neck quickly and backing up.

The mischief in her light brown eyes carried with it a seduction that I knew all too well. Before I could respond one way or the other, I was suddenly mobbed on both sides by squealing teenage girls demanding my attention. I quickly downed the rest of my champagne, and passed Danielle my empty glass, before letting my daughters pull me off to a corner of the room.

"Welcome Home Daddy!" Cyn squeals.

"Yeah, Welcome Home Pops," Lia said.

I hugged both of them to me and fought the tears in my throat because I didn't want anyone to see me cry. Spending 18 years inside had made my relationship with my 18-year-old and 19-year-old incredibly strained, but the love was still there no matter what differences we had, the love out-weighed it.

"Damn, what the fuck you 2 been eating?" I asked stepping back so that I could look at them from head to toe.

The similarities between the 2 were uncanny and scary as shit, considering they had different mothers. Both were similarly built at about 5'7, 160+ lbs. and they had the same smooth flawless chocolate skin that was like black coffee with a splash of cream.

Cyn was the girly girl type with her nails done, lashes on fleek, and a show-stopping hair do to match. Lia dressed according to her sexual orientation, and since it was obvious that she liked girls, it was appropriate that she had on some jeans with a black Ninja Turtle t-shirt. They were my kids, my only two, similar yet completely different.

"Aye pop, you know I hardly eat…. Food anyway," Lia said laughing.

14

"Eww, girl shut up," Cyn said playfully, pushing her sister.

It made my heart beat faster to see them two interacting because they had just found out about each other only a year ago. Lia's birth mom had kept her a secret from me and had lied consistently to her, but the truth always has a way of coming out. I'd loved Lia from the day I'd found out about her, but Cyn had been resistant at first. They were well past that now.

"So, daddy what are you gonna do now that you're out? Cyn asked.

"Stay out," I replied simply.

"I heard that shit," Lia mumbled.

"Well, I and Lia were talking, and we decided that you've got about 72 hours to yourself, and then we get your undivided attention, agreed?" Cyn asked, sticking her hand out.

It was already clear to see why Cyn's mom had said she was destined to be a judge or trial lawyer.

"Are you in on this too?" I asked, cutting my eyes at Lia.

"It's a package deal pops."

I chuckled and shook my head, but I also shook my daughter's hand.

"Nice doing business with you old man, I'll see you in 3 days," Cyn said, kissing me swiftly on the cheek before disappearing back into the crowd.

"I gotta run too pops, my girl is waiting on me."

"Where is Miss Imani anyways?" I asked.

Lia turned towards the crowd of people who were making plates of food, talking loud and dancing like my momma's tiny apartment was a country club venue. Once she spotted who she was looking for, she pointed her out. Imani was a cute lil brown skin chick and based on what Lia had told me about her, I felt like their love and loyalty were real.

"Why does she look so scared?" I asked laughing.

"This is the first time she's been around the family, and you know how that can be."

"Yeah, I get it because these bunch of muthafuckas are *CRAZY*, and they bout to get loose when that liquor fly," I replied, chuckling and looking with love at my dysfunctional crew.

"That's *exactly* why I'm about to shake the spot. I'll call you later though. Love you pops."

"Love you one," I said giving her another hug and then watching as she went to get her girl.

The evident relief that sprang up on Imani's face was comical, but I knew she'd get the hang of us.

"Here you go bruh," Byrd said, passing me another flute of champagne, and hugging me.

"Thanks sis, and thanks for getting everyone together. It's good to be loved by family."

"You know I gotchu bro-ham! Of course, you know there are a few renegade bitches here, but I didn't invite them," she said quickly.

At first, I'd thought that she was talking about my ex-girl Danielle until I followed her line of sight. The person I saw holding up the wall a few feet away was so unexpected that I almost dropped my glass on the floor.

"Why is my ex-wife here?" I mumbled, hoping against hope she wasn't reading my lips.

"Bruh you know *damn well* that I didn't invite her so that must mean that your daughter did."

I immediately started searching the crowd, but I didn't spot my daughter Cyn anywhere and I know why her ass had vanished on purpose. As surprised as I was to see Mercedes,

I was even more thrown off that my mom had let her in the house. My entire family blamed her for me having to do more time because even though I'd gone in with 10 years for two-gun charges, I'd got more time for her bringing me dope. I hadn't asked her to bring me a damn thing, but one day she showed up with a pussy full of heroin and the drug dog had sat down on her. I was beyond furious when I was hauled to the hole for trying to introduce contraband into the penal system, that anger bled away to fury when I realized that unless I wanted my daughter to lose both of her parents, I was gonna have to take the street charge that was sure to follow.

So, I did, and I earned myself ten more years just for being a good guy to a dumb bitch. Even now as I stared dispassionately into her brown eyes, I *knew* that *she knew* what I was thinking.

"Don't stress that shit L-Boogie, you are home now and that's all that matters."

"You're right. You're absolutely mufucking right!" I replied, tipping my champagne flute to my lips and quickly guzzling the contents.

"Come on, I got something for you."

I sat my glass down and followed my sister into the crowd. We danced our way from one side of the room to the other, and somewhere in between, I ended up with a plate loaded down with all my favorites. It had been years since I'd eaten pork, but the BBQ ribs sitting on top of the macaroni and cheese had my mouth watering. By the time we made it down the hallway to my mother's room, I had one rib in between my teeth, attacking it like a dog that had gotten used to fighting for his food.

"Don't worry my nigga, I made sure the ribs were beef. Not that you bothered to ask," Byrd said, glancing at me over her shoulder and laughing.

"Shut up," I said, around a mouth full of food.

When we got to the back bedroom, Byrd closed the door, and then pulled a big Ziploc bag from under her shirt. Seeing all that green made me pass her my plate with quickness. I kept the bag of weed close to my nose without actually opening it, wanting to savor every moment before liftoff.

"What strand is this?" I asked.

"It's an Indica hybrid strand of Kush called watermelon grape ape, and this shit is *lethal*."

"How lethal?" I asked, smiling.

She put my plate aside for a moment and pulled her loner stoner peace pipe out of her pocket.

"Take it for a spin my nigga but keep your seatbelt on and your hands inside the vehicle at all times," she said, passing me the pipe and her lighter.

I swiftly packed the bowl like I hadn't missed a day and fired up without hesitation. With the first hit, I knew I was in trouble because my lungs sent the mayday signal to my brain. One would think that would absolutely stop me from taking another hit, but if you thought that, then you didn't know Leroy Bly. I hit that bitch again, and suddenly, the pipe jumped out of my hand. Byrd's instant laughter and her quick reaction time of catching the pipe told me that this shit had happened before.

I tried to swallow the smoke, but it was too much like being in a house fire. I choked and coughed until the delicious tasting rib I'd just inhaled before the weed tried to run back up my throat the way that kids do sliding boards in playgrounds. It took great effort for me to keep it down, but I did.

"That shit hit hard, like back taxes my nigga," she said, laughing openly at my struggle to get my life together.

"Is this real weed?"

"Yeah, but you get high as shit super-fast like smoking that synthetic marijuana, right?" She asked.

"Hell yeah," I replied, stumbling to my mom's bed and sitting down beside my plate.

"This was the first strain that I and mom used for the baked brownies."

"N-no wonder both food trucks are doing so well. You got that Mike Tyson!" I said, still struggling to breathe as the high intensified.

A soft knock at the door had both of us looking stupid. Byrd picked up the weed off the floor and tossed it to me while stuffing her pipe back in her jeans pocket as she stepped to the door. As soon as she opened it my eyes locked with Mercedes over top of Byrd's 5ft. height.

When Byrd looked at me with a question in her eyes, I smiled but shook my head no. The question had been, "did I need her to put her 168lbs of ass-whooping on my baby's mother?" The high part of me almost said yeah just because I wanted to see if Mercedes still had that Maryland hood bitch inside her. I knew that despite her having a 7-inch height advantage on my sister, they were evenly matched with the hands, but this wasn't the time and place for fuck shit.

"I'ma go holla at mom really quick," Byrd said.

I nodded, but my eyes stayed glued to Mercedes. I was surprised to see that she had dreadlocks that flowed to her waist, but they looked good on her. I wasn't about to tell her no shit like that though. From the looks of things, she'd lost every bit of 200lbs, and her coca-cola shape was jumping like high school homecoming. Again, something else I wasn't about to tell her. I really didn't have shit to say to her, but I would hear her out since she was here. When the door closed behind Byrd, I'd expected Mercedes to start talking, but she just stood there looking at me.

"Say whatever you came to say," I demanded.

"I came to apologize, and to ask you to forgive me."

"Not in this lifetime, huh?"

I wasn't paying attention to her words as much as I was paying attention to the pretty black sig saver 9mm she'd pulled out of nowhere.

"Well maybe in the next lifetime then sweety," she said, raising the gun from her side.

I was too shocked to move, and part of me was praying this was a hallucination brought on by some really good weed. Within seconds I was looking down the barrel of the gun and I wanted to scream, but I couldn't. I mentally braced for impact, but my brain quickly registered that the gun was still moving upwards. It stopped directly under her chin, and before I could utter a word, I saw the top of her dreads part so that her brain could squeeze through. The actual sound of the pistol going off seemed to have a ten-second delay, but I couldn't hear it over the screaming anyways. It took me a while to realize that I was the one screaming.

Chapter 3
2027

"Welcome home L," Amelia said, opening the door to my four-bedroom house before I could put the key in.

"Don't come outside without your mask on, you know we can't have anyone catching covid," I replied stepping inside and closing the door.

"Where's Byrd?" Candice asked, coming out of the kitchen carrying a tumbler with white Hennessy in it.

I pulled my mask off while accepting the glass she handed me and took a quick gulp.

"She had to get home and take Clay to work, why?"

"I was just asking bae," Candice replied softly.

I could tell by her tone that I'd hurt her feelings, which hadn't been my intention. The stress I felt was something we'll all render because we were a family, so Gini being locked up hurt us all.

"Has she called yet?" I asked,

"Not yet bae, but I made dinner in case you wanted to eat while we wait," Candice offered.

"Or we can do something else to distract you," Amelia said, stepping towards me until she was peering up into my face.

Her baby blue eyes were alight with mischievous intent behind the round frames of her glasses. When I glanced up at Candice, I saw the same expression, which made me chuckle as I threw back the remainder of the potent liquor. Amelia and Candice were slight opposites in physical appearance, but they were alike in every other way. Amelia's skin was what you describe as milky white, but against her reddish-brown hair, it was sexy.

Candice on the other hand was my warm chocolate complexion, and she tasted just as sweet. The best part was that they were both freaks in their own way, and there were few limits. Amelia was the taller of the two standing at 5'4, with Candice bringing up the rear at 5'1. Anybody who knew about my three wives knew that my type was short, thick, big titties with a matching ass, and preferably bi-sexual.

"You two didn't play while I was gone?"

"No *daddy*," they replied in unison.

They both knew that I was okay with them fucking each other because we were one big family, but most of the time, they insisted on me being in the middle. Amelia's impatience flared, and without another word, she unzipped my jeans so that she could pull my dick out. She looked me squarely in the eye while slowly stroking it and challenging me with her defiance.

They both knew that I was in control *always* unless I said otherwise, but moments like this were what I lived for. Amelia took a tiny step back, but she didn't let my dick go, nor did she break eye contact. Her next step was a little bigger, but it became obvious what she was doing, which was leading me. I held out my glass and Candice took it, and then I let Amelia pull me gently into the living room. Once she had me there, she took a seat on my right and waited patiently for her partner in crime while continuing to stroke my dick to life.

"Do you want the honey or chocolate syrup?" Candice asked, holding one in each hand.

"Um, you start with the honey, and I'll finish with the chocolate," Amelia replied, smiling seductively.

The game they were playing was dangerous for me, but all was fair in love and war. Candice sat down on my left and then they both leaned down and kissed my dick simultaneously. They shared a quick kiss with each other which only made my dick harder as I watched, and then the games began. Candice raised the bottle of honey and tipped it until the beautiful gold drizzled over the head of my dick and slid slowly down my shaft.

"Damn that's sexy," I mumbled, leaning back on the couch and putting my arms out so that I could massage both of their asses.

I heard Candice moan softly as she opened her mouth wide and dove on my dick like an Olympic medalist. The back of her throat became my home, and she welcomed me over and over and over again. While she did her thing, Amelia watched with rapt attention like a runner waiting on the baton to be passed. After a few minutes of deep throat action, Candice came up for air, allowing Amelia time to drizzle some chocolate syrup on me. Before the sugary dark liquid could reach my shaft, Amelia was sucking and slurping on my dick like her ice cream was melting.

They were both skilled with their mouths even though they had different styles. While Candice had taken the direct approach of me boxing with her tonsils, Amelia took her time and alternated between sucking the head and licking the shaft. When she finally took my dick all the way into her mouth, my eyes rolled into the back of my head. The sudden ringing of the phone had me looking around with one eye open, but Candice was already moving to get it. A few moments later, the cordless phone was in my hand, and I could hear the sound of breathing.

"What's up baby?" I asked. "How did you know it was me?" Gini asked.

"Because we go through the same routine after every visit," I replied, smiling.

"Don't be acting like you know me L, because you don't," she said, but I could hear the smile in her voice.

"I *DO* know you, my wife, just like you know me."

"Uh huh, which means you're probably getting your dick sucked right now. Which one is doing it, Amelia or Candice?"

"Th-They're taking turns, but right now it's Amelia," I replied, fighting to breathe at a normal rate.

"Well, she better slows down baby because I can tell that you're almost there. Make them switch because you know Candice doesn't like for you to cum in her mouth, let's test your restraint."

"You're *killing* me Gini," I replied, grabbing a fistful of Amelia's hair and pulling her away from her meal.

Instead of assuming her original position, Candice kneeled in front of me and took my dick into her mouth while staring up into my eyes lovingly.

"Oh shit," I mumbled.

"She's deep throating that dick ain't she baby?" Gini asked huskily.

"Mmmm Hmmm."

"Good, now close your eyes and imagine it was me. Picture my soft, juicy lips taking you all the way to the back of my throat without gagging. See the love and passion in my eyes as I pray for your soul to leave your body with every movement of my mouth."

"Oh f-fuck," I moaned, reaching blindly for Candice's braids.

I could feel Amelia moving around beside me, and then I felt her lips on mine. Her kiss held hunger and passion while giving me the skills of her tongue in another way. In my ear, I could hear Gini's soft breathing becoming more labored, and I knew that she was playing with her pussy right now. That knowledge only made my dick throb harder.

"I love you so, so much Leroy," Gini whispered.

"I love you too baby."

"God, I wish you were inside me right now. I don't care if that dick splits me wide open, I *still* wanna ride it baby," Gini said passionately.

"You will baby, I promise that you will."

As her breathing continued getting heavier in my ear, I knew that her own climax wasn't far off. I quickly pulled Candice's head up, and Amelia dropped right back into position. Candice moved back up beside me and started kissing me while I wrapped my fingers up in Amelia's hair so that I could guide her every move.

"B-Babe, I wanna cum! Are you ready for me to cum for you?" Gini asked breathlessly.

"Mmmm Hmmm," I mumbled, never pausing my kiss with Candice increasing Amelia's speed.

"Lee-Lee-Leroy!" Gini panted, and I knew she was cumming.

My teeth sunk into Candice's bottom lip, as I let Amelia's head go so that she could start swallowing all the cum that I was filling her mouth with. Amelia gagged once but kept right on sucking while Gini moaned her satisfaction in my ear. It took forever for the world to stop spinning, and I regained my footing. I could taste Candice's blood in my mouth. When I looked at her, she just smiled and took the phone from me.

"Sis? He just bit my lip until it bled, and Amelia almost choked on all the cum pumping down her throat! What the hell did you say to him?"

I couldn't hear Gini's response, but Candice laughed hard before passing me the phone back.

"Come on Milly, we've got a job to do," she said, holding her hand out to Amelia.

I was about to ask what the hell they had going on, but I could hear Gini calling me.

"I'm here babe, what's up?"

"I just wanted you to know how much I love and appreciate you L, for real. You make me happier than anyone in the world ever could babe."

"You're always so soft after you orgasm, you pussy," I said.

We both laughed but when the laughter died, the silence became deafening.

"Get out of your head baby," I said gently.

"I'm trying L, you know I am."

"But?" I asked when she stopped speaking.

"Sometimes it feels so hopeless in here."

She didn't have to say more than that because I was a veteran at doing time, and I knew *all about* that hopelessness. It was worse than any pandemic that had ever hit the planet, and twice as contagious if you weren't strong in the mind. This knowledge was why I got up every morning with the determination to fight this beast alongside my wife. I would forever be her anchor in the storm.

"I got you baby, you know that right?" I asked.

"Yeah, I know, and that's why I ain't giving up, we're just fighting a different fight."

"Exactly, now ain't the time to give up because our date with Destiny is approaching fast, " I said.

"I know it is baby… the phone is about to hang up, but I'll call you tonight sometime. I love you, Leroy."

"And I love you right back sweetheart."

When the phone clicked in my ear, I closed my eyes and swallowed my pain to keep from screaming. The dull ache was nothing new because I'd felt it from the moment Gini had told me her release date. Having done my fair share behind the razor wire and bright lights, I was used to hearing all types of numbers when it came to the sentences the state of VA handed out. Getting 1200 years just for being in the wrong place at the wrong time had sounded completely the fuck insane though! That had been my opinion before I fell in love with her beautiful personality, but once that love and loyalty were cemented, her sentence became unacceptable.

We'd spent the last 5 years, and the better part of a million dollars, trying to legally obtain her freedom. So far, there had been nobody to give us a clear path for what we wanted, and for that reason, my patience was *done done*. I'd married Gini legally knowing not only what I was up against, but also knowing what I was prepared to do about it. I wouldn't just catch a grenade-like Bruno Mars, I'd throw a couple of my damn self.

"Daddy, you have to come with us. Gini's orders," Candice said.

I looked up to find both her and Amelia standing in front of me, naked and unafraid. In all honesty, I wasn't feeling up to the reindeer games they wanted to play, but I stood up because Gini would want me to. They both quickly undressed me, and then led me into the master bathroom. Once we entered, I immediately knew what was going on because the water was full in my jacuzzi tub, and there were tons of scented bubbles covering the surface.

"Amelia, you got this," Candice said, letting my hand go, and leaving the room.

Amelia led me over to the tub, climbed in, and held out her hand to me. I followed her lead and sat down in between her open thighs. She wasted no time lathering a sponge and gently bathing me with the finesse of a skilled nurse. I closed my eyes and leaned against her while imagining that these were Gini's thick thighs, I was relaxing in between, with every moment of the sponge in Amelia's hand, I could feel my dick coming to life again, yet my hunger was for the smile I could see on the backs of my eyelids.

"For you, my king," Candice said.

I opened my eyes to find her standing just outside of the tub with a plate balanced in one hand and a bottle of red wine in the other. When I nodded approvingly, she stepped into the tub with us and sat directly across from me. Once she handed me the wine, she swiftly maneuvered around in the water until she was sitting with her back up against me. I could see that my steak cooked to medium, the way that I like it, and she'd cut it up alongside my mashed potatoes. She began feeding me over her shoulder, while Amelia continued to bathe me sensually. Even as I chewed thought-fully, viewing my lifestyle from an outsider's perspective, I knew that any nigga would envy me. By all accounts, I had everything that any man could want, but I wasn't *just* any man, I was Leroy, muthafucking Bly! And I wanted it *all*!

Chapter 4
2022

"Leroy! Leroy are you alright?! Leroy, open the door!" Byrd insisted, pounding on the flimsy wood harder than she had in the last 5 minutes.

There were no sounds of music coming from the living room, nor could I hear anyone talking, which made me feel somewhat better. As soon as I'd gathered myself enough to stop screaming like a frightened schoolgirl, I'd shot Byrd a text and told her to clear mom's house *right the fuck now* because we had a life and death situation. My sister knew me well enough to know that I wasn't the type to overly exaggerate shit, so within minutes, I heard my mom's apartment go silent. Following that, were the sounds of people leaving, but not before they grabbed a to-go plate.

All this while, I'd been sitting on my mom's bed, staring at the glassy-eyed expression on Mercedes' dead face. I wanted to do the respectful thing and close her eyes, but the truth was that I'd seen one too many Cop shows to fuck with a dead body. My mind was already in survival mode, trying to figure out how to pull a magic trick so that I could say I was *never here*! Unfortunately, this was real life, not make-believe, and I couldn't just undo this shit right here. Dead or alive, Mercedes always seemed to put me in a trick bag!

"Yo, L, come on bruh, you gotta open the door because mom is getting worried," Byrd said.

This message was delivered in her normal tone of voice, but I clearly heard the message beneath her words. The last thing that I wanted was for my mom to have another stroke, and I *damn sure* didn't want it to be my fault. I straightened my spine as I stood up and walked over to the door. I gently pulled it open enough for Byrd to squeeze through into the room, and then I closed it again.

"*ohhhhh shittt,*" Byrd whispered.

I turned around to find her standing a few feet away with her hands up to her mouth, and her gaze fixed on Mercedes.

"My sentiments exactly."

"Bro, what *happened*?" she asked.

I quickly ran down the events that led to this situation, and by the time I was done, she was sitting on the bed fumbling with the bag of weed. I desperately wanted the intense feeling from the high earlier, but that shit had vanished as quick as Mercedes' life, and I knew I needed a clear mind right now. It took Byrd a couple of times before she got the pipe loaded and sparked, but after her second inhale, I saw her visibly relax, not by much though.

"What the fuck am I supposed to do?" I asked.

"There's really only one thing that you can do at this point, call the cops."

"Are you out of your *damn mind*?! Do you really think that the cops are gonna believe the story I gotta tell?" I asked.

"I feel what you're saying Bruh but trying to hide this shit will only make you look worse. You have nothing to fear because you know that you didn't do anything wrong."

"Since when the fuck has me not doing anything wrong ever stopped me from getting the raw end of the deal?" I asked seriously.

"You've got a point L, but now that you told me what happened, I can look at everything and see it. I'm not trained for that shit, but you know damn well that the cops are, and they will clearly see that she did this shit to herself. Trust me bruh, you're good."

I stared at Byrd hard for a few moments wondering just how high she was right now. I'd never doubted my little sister for any reason, and that wasn't a decision that I would ever regret. Which meant, if it wasn't broke then, why fuck with it. I reluctantly pulled my phone out of my pocket and dialed 911. The whole time the phone was ringing, I could feel the bile rising in my throat, but by the time someone answered on the other end, I'd figured out how to talk around it. I gave a clear, detailed description of what happened and then I hung up.

Since my mother's apartment was on the border between D.C. and Maryland, it was a shot in the dark as to who would respond to the call. Either way, I knew it was time to clean up.

"Yo Byrd, you gotta stash the weed, and this," I said, pulling my ringer .45 from the small of my back.

"My nigga, what the fuck are you doing with a gun?"

"We can have that conversation later slim, right now it's all hands on deck," I replied.

The way she snatched the gun from my hand let me know that her attitude was real, but my mind was on the sounds of apparent sirens. My run-ins with law enforcement were countless, but I would *never* feel at ease in their presence. Even if I'd done nothing. Byrd quickly disappeared into our mom's closet and emerged a few moments later still shaking her head in obvious frustration. I wasn't one to seek approval from anyone, not even from my sister, but I understood that she thought I'd lost my damn mind considering I'd just done a bid for guns. What she didn't understand was that once you'd done as much time as I had, you would rather die than go back. That meant if shit hit the fan, then I was holding court in the streets.

"I'ma go warn mom that we're about to be invaded, just sit on the bed and act natural," she said.

We made eye contact and suddenly burst into spontaneous laughter over her comments. I was still wiping the tears from my eyes as I sat down next to my plate of cold, and forgotten, food while she carefully stepped around the body of my ex, I did my best to avoid eye contact, but in the end, I couldn't resist staring at her wasted beauty because I was still trying to understand what had led Mercedes to this moment.

I knew exactly how rough her childhood had been, including the time she'd spent captive in a sex trafficking ring. Not even that had broken her, so the thought that my lack of forgiveness had pushed her over the edge just didn't make sense. This shit was all too weird to process, and I knew that wasn't due to the slight weed buzz that was lingering over my subconscious. The sound of banging on my mom's apartment door caused me to jump involuntarily, and I could suddenly feel the blood in my veins slow down like rush hour traffic.

Despite having done *absolutely nothing,* I was still nervous enough to feel the cramps in my stomach from the shit pains that were coming on. All this anxiety wasn't slowing up my thought process though. I quickly pulled out my phone and took a few quick pictures of Mercedes, how she was positioned and where the gun was laying. I sent the pix to my cloud account, while simultaneously shooting them to my lawyer's office. By the time the first cop was entering my mom's bedroom door open, I'd shot the necessary text to explain the pictures, and my phone was back in my pocket.

"Let me see your hands sir," the cop demanded, already unsnapping his gun holster so that he could rest his hand on the rubber grip of his Glock .40.

I raised my hands nice and slow, but I didn't stand up because that hadn't been part of the instructions. I waited patiently for the rest of the cops to enter the room while keeping my focus on maintaining steady breathing so that an unexpected asthma attack didn't result in an ass whooping, or worse.

"Are you the one that called?" A tall black cop, with gold lieutenant's bars on his jacket, asked.

"Yes, sir,' I replied.

He motioned for me to get up and follow him out of the room. When I stepped out into the hallway, all I saw were black-uniformed D.C. police and the crime scene unit team. I made sure to keep my hands up high enough for everyone to see, and I made eye contact with no one. The lieutenant led me all the way outside to his car, where we stopped, and he pulled out a pack of cigarettes.

"You smoke these, or just weed?"

"Nah, I'm good," I replied, answering cautiously.

"Relax, weed is completely legal within the District of Columbia. I want you to tell me your version of what happened and start with your name."

I glanced at the nameplate on his jacket and saw that his name was Hogan. Lt. Steve Hogan. Something in my brain screamed that he was familiar to me somehow, but I pushed that aside and spit out the facts that I'd listed in my 911 call. By the time I was done, Hogan had finished smoking his entire cigarette, and he was simply leaning against his police cruiser staring at me hard. I knew the stare; I'd seen it a thousand times on the inside. He didn't believe the shit I was saying.

"So, what you're telling me is that your ex-wife killed herself because you wouldn't forgive her?" He asked slowly.

"Yes Sir."

"She orphaned 5 kids all because you wouldn't *FOR-GIVE HER?*" He asked w/ obvious disbelief. I opened my mouth to answer yes for the third fucking time when his actual question caught up to my already racing mind. I hadn't said a damn thing about how many kids Mercedes had, and the fact that this cop *KNEW* that info had me looking at him with my head cocked to the side.

"Who are you?" I asked.

He slowly reached his right hand up and tapped his name tag slowly, while smirking at me. I looked at it again to make sure that I hadn't misread it, and I hadn't, but wherever this nigga was in my memory banks was currently inaccessible to me. When I looked back up at him, I really studied his face. The brown skin complexion and curly hair hinted at mixed heritage somewhere in his bloodline. His age was hard to discern because black don't crack, but the slight gray at his temples and in his goatee told me we were from the same generation.

There was no doubt that because of his size alone, I should've remembered him because 6'5, 300lbs was a nice weight for some smoke if he wanted it. Ultimately though, it was his plain brown eyes that told me my instincts about him knowing either me, Mercedes, or both of us in another lifetime was real, right, and exact.

"Like I said Lieutenant, my ex-wife died by her own hand and there was nothing I could do to stop her."

"Except for forgiving her," he replied quickly.

"God is the one who forgives, not me."

"Be sure to remember that when the gun is aimed at you," he said, pointing two fingers at me.

"Lieutenant Hogan, we need you," someone called.

He swiftly pulled out a pair of handcuffs and motioned for me to turn around. I started to say fuck nah and see what this big nigga was built like, but I saw my daughters in my mind's eye. That kept me calm. I turned my back to him and allowed him to handcuff me before putting me in the back of his car.

"Sit tight," he said, shutting the door.

I watched him walk away with mounting fury, but the moment I saw Byrd come out of the apartment building, I found my reserve of hope. She said something to the passing lieutenant, but he ignored her and kept right on moving. I could read her frustration, but she shook that shit off, and immediately started searching for me. As soon as she spotted me, we locked eyes and she ran over to the car.

"Now see, this right here is some bullshit bruh, but I got you don't even worry bout it," she said, pulling her phone out.

I watched her tapping the screen with lightning speed, and then she bent down so that she and I were in the Insta-gram frame together.

"I want you all to look at this shit! I mean *really* look at it because it's *all the way* fucked up! They got my big brother in the back of a goddamn cop car because a bitch decided to end her life in front of him. Someone *please* tell me how the fuck they can lock up this righteous black man for the crime of.....Not a *muthafuckin* thing! When are the cops gonna stop abusing their fucking power out here?! We gotta do something, and we gotta do it *now!*"

When she put the phone down and started typing again, I smiled with pride because the woman that my baby sister had become was an amazing force of nature to see in action.

"Call my lawyer sis," I said.

"What's her number?"

I quickly recited the number for her and waited impatiently for her to explain what was happening. A short 5 minutes later, she hung up and smiled through the window at me.

"You're a smart man my dude because sending those pictures was *GENIUS*! Christie Leary is a top-notch attorney, and she said that you know that so just chill, she got this."

"Let's hope so," I said.

Movement coming from the front of my mom's building got my attention, and the next thing I knew, the corner was pulling out a stretcher covered by a white sheet. For the first time, a wave of sadness actually hit me, and I caught a flash of Mercedes' smile in my mind. Knowing that I was never gonna see it again put a lump in my throat, but I swallowed it because I knew I'd have to be stronger than ever for my daughter Cyn. Her mom was her whole world, and now that world was forever rocked.

"Here comes that bitch ass lieutenant," Byrd said, already pointing her phone in his direction.

I could see that he was occupied by his own phone call, but the grit on his face told me that he knew he was being filmed. He walked straight up on my sister, almost like he intended to punch her in the face, but instead, he asked her nicely to step aside. Once she did, he pulled the back door and hauled me out. Without a word, he took the cuffs off of me and spun me around to face him.

"I'll see you soon Leroy."

The look in his eyes was one of determination and definite hostility, but I still didn't understand why. Instead of asking questions, I hugged my sister and told her to tell mom I love her, but I had to go. My steps weren't hurried, but they were purposeful as I strode to my black 2021 Dodge Charger. Once I slid behind the wheel and started the engine, I eased out of the parking lot. I was crossing the Woodrow

Wilson bridge seven minutes later doing 92mph, listening to the sounds of MoneyBaggYo preach thru my speakers.

The moment I hit the Virginia side of the bridge, I reduced my speed, but it wasn't fast enough because I saw the cop tucked off in the corner with the radar light showing. The speedometer said I was doing 77mph, which was typical traffic flow, but I could already see the flashing blue lights in my rearview. The relief that I felt at not having my gun on me caused me to smile as I pulled over by the exit for Alexandria, Virginia. I waited patiently for the cop to come to my window, but when I saw his shadow appear and I looked, I saw something I didn't wanna see.

"Shut the car off and keep your hands where I can see them, Bly. You're under arrest!"

Aryanna

Chapter 5
2027

When my eyes opened, I knew that it wasn't the alarm on my nightstand that had awakened me, nor was it either one of the women curled up together sleeping beside me. It was Gini. My internal alarm moved when she moved, and when I read 5:30 am on my clock, I knew that my wife had just been made to stand for count. I couldn't explain how or when we'd become so in sync in every way, but we were blessed enough to feel each other no matter where we were in the world. She was my twin flame, and I was her light in the darkness.

Knowing that there was no more sleep to be had for me pushed me from beneath my warm comforter and sent me in search of a hot shower. Last night's pampering session had led to me having to thoroughly fuck both Candice and Amelia, which made my shower necessary because smelling like pussy all day would only have me distracted. I spent a quick 15 minutes beneath the blistering needles of heat shooting down from overhead, and by then, I was wide awake.

After drying myself off, I made sure to reenter my bed-room and dress quietly so that I didn't wake my wives. A dark blue-black billionaire button-up, some black billionaire slacks, and matching black billionaire loafers completed that task, and after I grabbed my Glock.27, I was out the door. Business was my focus and for that reason, I chose to drive my dark green 2028 GMC Denali. My first stop was McDonalds to grab myself a sausage, egg, and cheese McGriddle because I'd learned the hard way that hungry diabetics don't think straight.

I sat in the parking lot and polished off my sandwich and hash brown so that I could take my medication and get on the move. A search of all of my cars was guaranteed to turn up with two things; weed, and all my necessary medications because I needed both to survive. When I was done with my medicine, I sparked a pre-rolled blunt of pink diamond Kush, turned up the old YoGotti I kept in rotation, and my day finally began. My first few hours were spent riding around checking on all the food trucks that I owned that were stationed all over Washington D.C, and once that was done, I swung past my restaurant on the Northwest side of the city.

Because I'd had the good sense to make my sister my business partner, all of my businesses ran smoother than a Rolex, but I still liked to see for myself how my millions were made. It was the hustla in me. Despite owning seven food trucks, two marijuana dispensaries, a restaurant, a publishing company, and a tow truck company, I didn't really have an office per se. I did my business on the move so that I could be anywhere at any time. At 7:15 am, my phone started ringing throughout the truck, and the thought of business went out the window. I answered immediately and hit the necessary buttons to bring my baby's voice to me.

"Good morning my beautiful wife."

"You sound *WAY* too awake right now baby. Did my sister wives not do their job?"

Her questions made me laugh out loud as I was shaking my head.

"I mean, you know they came out to play but my dick game is upper techelon! Leroy junior *always* delivers that pot of gold at the end of the rainbow!"

This time, it was her melodic laughter that filled my truck, and it made me smile to hear it.

"L, you're an *arrogant* mufucka! I swear it's a good thing you're ugly because if you were a pretty boy, you'd probably take over the world and make us call you Caesar."

"Nah, you can just call me Daddy. Daddy Dope Dick has a nice ring to it," I said

"You ain't gotta tell me twice baby because I'm hooked, and I ain't even *had* that big black mufucka inside me yet!"

"Don't worry baby, we're gonna fix that *real* soon, and I promise to have you a good *obgyn* on standby in case you need staples," I replied, laughing.

"Fuck you! I done already *told you* that you better not split my pussy open! This mufucka is so pretty and pink that if you split me open, you're gonna be mad at yourself, I promise."

"I believe you baby, and you know that I'll be as gentle as I can with you. What's your safe word again?" I asked, still laughing

"It's *fuck you*, you asshole!" she replied laughing too.

The sudden sound of another call coming in had me looking at my dashboard to see who was interrupting us.

"Babe, the lawyer is calling me, do you want me to merge her in?"

I could sense her nervousness in the way she hesitated, but I'd never admit that my stomach dropped too.

"Sure babe merge it," she replied.

I hit 2 buttons and crossed my fingers while taking a calming breath.

"Hello?"

"Hey Leroy, this is Natasha, and I have Christie, and Gini on the line for you. Wait one moment please."

"Ok," I replied quickly, after a few seconds of silence a different voice echoed throughout my truck.

"Good morning, Leroy, this is Christie Leary. How are you today?"

"I'm good Christie, and Gini is on the phone too."

"Ok perfect, Good morning, Virginia."

"Good morning, Christie."

"Well since I have you both here, that saves me the hassle of coordinating with the prison to speak with you Gini. So, I received word yesterday that Pony's mom will *NOT* be speaking on your behalf, nor will she give a written affidavit as to the abuse you suffered at her son's hand. Now, I know this is a complete 180 from what she'd said when I made initial contact with her, but apparently, Pony has a lawyer who's trying to help him get his sentence reduced as well.

Naturally, if his mother were to make statements against him, it would hurt his chances, and because of that, she's unwilling to help us. That's the bad news. The good news is that we still have all the documented evidence of his physical, emotional, mental and sexual abuse of you. So, we have plenty of ammo when it comes to showing that you were an unwilling participant in his crime spree. There's no reason to be discouraged because we already knew that this was an uphill battle," Christie said.

I could feel my jaw clenching and unclenching, and I knew without a doubt that Gini was fighting tears of frustration on the other end of the phone. My heart ached not to be able to hold her right now, but this news only strengthened my resolve that my wife would die a free woman, or I would die trying to free her.

"Thanks for the update, Christie please let me know if there's anything else I can do," I said.

"I absolutely will, and Virginia you just continue to hang in there, ok?"

"Ok," Gini replied hollowly.

"I'll talk to you two later," Christie said, disconnecting the call.

I quickly cleared the line, wishing with all my heart and soul that I could give my wife some form of comfort other than the words I was prepared to offer up. Words didn't really do shit for pain except mock it.

"Baby, listen, I-."

"L, I gotta go to work. I love you."

Before I could say anything else, I heard (Thank you for using GTL) and a resounding click. My anger flared white-hot, but not at Gini. My fury was strictly for the bitch made nigga that had put her in that hell hole she was forced to call home. Some people who knew Gini's story said it was nothing more than proof that karma was *real*, but to me, that was a one-dimensional approach to the situation. Had she left her ex-husband and three kids for the tall, dark, and mysterious neanderthal of a mechanic from around the corner? Yes, and did that same mechanic get her hooked-on crack, beat her, rape her, and get her unjustly sentenced to consecutive life sentences? Yes, again. But he also showed her a love *no one* had ever shown her, and that love gave birth to the hope that had grabbed my attention when I met her by chance.

Throughout my life, I'd heard people say that it was better to have loved and lost than to have not loved at all, and that's what Gini embodied for me. She was love and hope that grew from concrete with nothing but rainwater and sunlight for nourishment. To me, her beauty wasn't in the rose petals that she was made of, but in the thorns that protected her and still allowed her to grow even now. She was my beautiful savage, and that was my karma that I claimed proudly.

Knowing that she was crying at this very moment had my heart beating fast enough to compete with the horsepower beneath my hood, and I knew what it was gonna take to calm me. I pulled a swift u-turn in the middle of the street and pointed my truck in the direction of I-395. Once I was on the highway racing back to Virginia, I made a call that was necessary for the taste at hand.

"Yo, Demon, where you at?"

"I'm down here at the 7-11 off of Lockheed Blvd in Alexandria, what's rockin?"

"Stay there, I'm on my way," I replied, hanging up.

I quickly imputed the destination into my truck's GPS, but the 35-minute arrival time was unacceptable, so I pressed the gas closer to the floor, with every mile that passed, my mind became sharper, and I was able to visualize the moves I was planning to make. Proper planning had taken me to the top of the business world, but it had been embedded in me in the streets first. It was time to take it back there now, 20 minutes later, I slid my truck to a stop in front of the 7-11, and I waited for my dude to hop in. I could tell that he was high by the way he tried to maneuver his 6'0 ft, 250lbs into my truck backwards, but I didn't care because wherever I pointed, he would shoot without question.

"How much have you smoked today?" I asked, looking over at him.

"I only had 2 dippers bruh and I'm still thinking completely straight," he replied.

Smoking that *wett* was a big no, no in my lifestyle, and Demon knew that. At the same time, I knew no one could carry his baggage except for him, so me trying was powerless. I quickly pulled off while mentally calculating how long it was gonna take us to arrive at our destination.

"You're gonna be with me for the rest of the day, so let your sister know not to look for you," I said.

He pulled out his phone and made the call without any hesitation. While he did that, I pulled out another pre-rolled blunt and fired it up. I smoked half of it, and then I passed it to him. Trading one high for another wasn't smart on my part, but it served the purpose of keeping him occupied so that I could focus solely on the road in front of me. Once I noticed that he'd mellowed out and wasn't as jittery as when he'd first sat beside me, I turned the volume back up on my music. The two-hour drive to Roanoke Virginia only took an hour and a half and once I got there, I reached out to my nigga Leroy to get the right address; within 15 minutes, we were easing to a stop in front of a nice, white single-story home, with a small front yard and not a neighbor in sight for at least 6 blocks.

"What are we doing out here bruh?" he asked.

"Committing murder and saving lives."

Aryanna

Chapter 6
July 2022
(3 weeks later)

"Mr. Bly although, I understand that the death of your ex-wife was tragic, and officially ruled a suicide, I don't like the fact that you were mixed up in this after just being released from prison, with that being said, I'm gonna uphold the probation violation issued by your P.O. and I remand you to the Virginia Department of Corrections for the next 24 months. Make better decisions upon your release because if I see you again, I won't be so understanding."

The judge swiftly banged the gavel, and I knew that officially put his ruling in the books. I was stuck in prison for another 2 years. I waited patiently for the screen on the TV to go dark in the courtroom before I stood up and made my exit from my virtual hearing. I walked out of the makeshift classroom I'd been in and went directly to the Correctional Officer's desk to retrieve my ID card. The only good thing that came out of doing my hearings virtually was that I hadn't had to leave prison just to get the bad news delivered.

Covid-19 had everybody using two-week quarantine protocols, and at this point, that only added insult to injury, from the moment I'd hit Fairfax county adult detention center a few weeks back and called my lawyer, I knew that I was coming back to prison. The only unknown had been for how long. Mercedes' death wasn't what had me back in the general population currently walking up the sidewalk of Haynesville Correctional Center. It was the fact that I'd left the state of Virginia and crossed into D.C. without my P. O's permission.

A petty and technical violation, but a violation nonetheless that was punishable by incarceration. As I got closer to my building, I could feel my frustration give way to full-on anger because this was the *second* time that Mercedes' actions had caused me to be a guest of the state. If she were alive right now, I'd kill her monkey ass! I walked in the door and nodded at the cute redhead sitting in the control booth. On most days, seeing Correctional Officer Luna made me smile because she was one of the realists mufuckas working here, right now though I just wanted to lay in my rack, put my music on, and zone the fuck out.

"You ok Bly?" Luna asked.

"Yeah, I'm good slim, just got a lot on my mind."

"Well, I'm working late tonight, so come talk to me if you need to," she said sincerely.

I nodded and walked through the open door to my pod. I felt the heated stares from niggas who were jealous simply because their drip wasn't like mine, but I didn't spare them niggas a glance, instead, I headed for my bed area, *hating* the fact that I was in an open dorm right now. Out of my peripheral vision, I could see the bulk of a dude named Jerry heading in my direction at what he considered a fast pace.

"Not now Jerry," I said, dismissing his bullshit before his inflated jaws could open.

"I need the $400 you owe me L, or we got a problem."

Hearing this made me stop in my tracks instantly and give him my undivided attention. My brain instantly started analyzing his build looking for unknown weaknesses. We were about the same height, but aside from that, Jerry resembled a pregnant hippie with his neat ponytail and pot belly. If pigs could walk, I imagined that this was what they looked like, and since Jerry was a known snitch, we often referred to him as

"Fat 12."

Snitch or not though, he'd called me out and now he had to answer for that.

"Look, all I got is a couple of suboxone strips right now, but you can hold them for collateral until I send you a cash app later," I replied.

He nodded his head approvingly, and I motioned for him to follow me into the bathroom. When I glanced at the control booth, my eye briefly met Luna's and I subtly moved my head so that she would focus on the Pod on the other side of the building. She winked at me and rolled her chair away from the window. Right before I walked thru the swinging saloon-style doors of the pod bathroom, I locked eyes with my man Buckshot who was sitting on the phone. Buck had been down 20 years, and was an OG from Richmond, VA beyond the shadow of a doubt, so all it took was that look for him to understand the play. He smiled, said something into the phone's receiver, and then sat the phone on the back of the chair. All of this took mere seconds, and I had no doubt that Jerry was oblivious to all of it. Once I passed thru the bathroom doors, I continued walking to the second sink before turning around to face the lamb who'd come willingly to the slaughter.

"You know that I trust you L, it's just that-."

I silenced his bullshit by firing a hard swift jab at his nose, enjoying the sounds of his bones crunching. Before he could yell or run, I followed the left jab with my overhand right, and then I side-stepped to deliver a punishing left-handed uppercut. He hit his knees like a building collapsing, and the look in his eyes was more distant than my future release date. I know he was done, but I still grabbed him by his ponytail and used my knee to destroy his face even more. I didn't stop until I heard the murmurs behind me, and I finally released my grip so that he could topple to the floor.

The adrenaline coursing through my body had my brain on autopilot and it wasn't until I heard mufuckas behind me laughing that I realized my dick was in my hand, and I was pissing on my enemy on the floor.

"Yo, L, you crazy as shit," Buckshot said from behind me.

I shook my dick twice, tucked it back inside my jeans, and stepped to the sink to wash my hands.

"Tell his bitch ass friends to come get him Buck," I said.

I heard him laugh right before he hollered for 2 dudes named Edge and RC. When I came out of the bathroom, I could tell that the entire pod knew what had just happened, which meant my odds of getting caught were at 100% *minimum*. Human cameras worked better than the eye in the sky when it came to snitching, and most of the niggas in here were scared to fight. Just in case though, I looked at all the weak niggas in their eyes so that they knew I don't give a fuck. A nigga named Dee from Maryland tried to wear a smirk on his face like he was built for some shit, but everybody knew he was a petty thief, gay as fuck, and an overall bitch type. He must've thought that staring at me thru his short-ass dreadlocks was supposed to be intimidating, but he averted his gaze after a few seconds.

I started to fuck him up anyway, but I knew that it would be a hate crime because of his choice to suck dick. When I moved to go to my bed area, a nigga named Pie Face motioned for me to stop past his bed area, but I ignored that shit. Pie used to be a legend in the hood back home, but the years spent in prison had turned him into somebody the City of Manassas wouldn't recognize. Niggas all across the compound called him *captain* Pie Face because he stayed moving with the administration whenever he could. Every time I looked at him, I saw the meek niggas inheriting the earth, so for the most part, I kept my distance. A lot of dudes were cool with prison, but 85% of them same niggas would get smoked on the street.

"You good bruh?" Buck asked, tossing me a towel to dry my hands on.

"Yeah, I'm good. The judge upheld the violation time though."

"I figured that by the way you just whooped Jerry's bitch ass," he replied laughing.

"Bruh that nigga asked for that. I told him that I'd pay his fat, funky ass when I felt like it, but now he's beat both ways."

The look that Buck gave me just made me shake my head as I walked towards my bed area because he'd told me months ago that I wasn't gonna pay Jerry. In prison, your word was your bond, so I'd had every intention of paying him until he'd come out his mouth sideways and tried to carry me. I ain't never allowed a nigga to do that. Buck fell into step beside me because our beds were right next to each other. My nigga Buck was only 5'10, 230lbs, but niggas moved out of his way like he was some type of giant. He didn't have a little man complex; it was just that his reputation was larger than life. He was from Mosby, the Southside of one of Virginia's most dangerous cities, and just because he smiled a lot didn't mean he wouldn't blow your head off. He only smiled so that you could see his gold fronts.

"Yo E, you cooking tonight?" Buck asked.

"Only if it's me, you, and L,"E replied.

"Get whatever you need out of my box,"

I said, grabbing my JPs player off of my bed so that I could listen to music. I put my headphones on the top of my head, selected my Money BaggYo playlist, and headed for the phone. A couple of dudes tried to stop me so that they could holla at me, but I kept moving because I really wasn't for all the loose raps. What I *really* wanted was to smoke a blunt of Kush to the face, but I wouldn't do that while Luna was working. Most niggas didn't give a fuck, but respect was a two-way street between her and me even though I did wanna fuck the shit out of her.

I started to go towards the kiosk and check my email, but one look at the clock told me that my conference call with Angela had already begun. I went to the phone, quickly dialed my sister's number, and waited for her to answer. As soon as Byrd picked up, she wanted to know what happened, so I told her to merge the call with Angela calling from the women's prison so that I would only have to explain the shit once. After she did that, I ran everything down to them, not even trying to hide my frustration.

"Damn bruh, that's fucked up! I'ma hit your lawyer up while you're on the phone and find out what her move is. Go ahead and holla at ya friend," Byrd said.

"Aight sis. What's up Angela, how was your –."

"This ain't Angela, it's Gini."

For a split second, I could feel the confusion contorting my features, and then the lightbulb went off. Gini's real name was Virginia, and she was Angela's cellmate.

"What's up Gini, did she just pass you the phone?" I asked, bewildered.

"No, I've been on here the whole time so that I could tell you she'd gone to medical, but you started flapping your lips before I could say shit!"

"Are you *seriously* talking shit about my lips like you ain't got a pretty set of dick suckas?" I asked, glancing around and to make sure no one was listening to me.

Her laughter echoed back to me, and I suddenly felt something loosen in my chest.

"You're funny, and I like to suck dick, so I don't got a problem with my lips. Shit, they're good for eating pussy too, just ask about me," she replied.

"Oh wow, you moving like that in there. Should I be worried that Angela don't really want me for my dick or my tongue?"

"Well, if she don't it ain't my fault because-."

"Ugh *hell* no!" she said, serious as shit.

It was my turn to laugh, which surprised me because I didn't feel up to it until now.

"I'm sorry to hear about court L, that shit sucks."

"Thanks, but that shit ain't bout nothing. It'll be over before you know it," I replied.

"Is that what you tell all the chicks?"

I laughed loudly, and she joined right in with me. I'd never had more than a passing conversation with Gini before, and as this one progressed, I found myself wondering why that was.

"Your girl just came back in, so I'll pass her the phone, stay focused and –."

"Hang up and call me back," I blurted.

"Wh-what?"

I could hear both hesitation and confusion in the way she stuttered that one word, but I pressed anyway.

"I want you to hang up the phone, tell her I said to call at 8:30pm, and I want you to call me right back so that we can finish talking," I explained.

The other end of the phone went silent for a full 30 seconds, but I knew that she hadn't hung up the phone. Somehow, I could *feel* her energy, and it soothed something inside me.

"Hey Angela…."

"Yeah!"

"L said to call back tonight at 8:30...."

"No, I'm just trying to reach my sister before they do count..."

"Uh huh, no problem sweety."

I could hear Angela saying something to Gini as she walked away, and Gini laughed. It wasn't like when we'd laughed though because that had been genuine.

"L, are you there?" Gini whispered into the receiver.

"Yeah, I'm here."

"Are you sure about this?" she asked skeptically.

"Absolutely."

"Ok L, but this is crazy, remember that."

Chapter 7
2027

"Go around back and wait for me to let you in, act like you're supposed to be here," I ordered, hopping out of my truck.

Demon followed my lead, and we approached the quiet house like we'd done it a million times before. The owner of the house was Pony's mother, but intel from my tech-savvy partner Lewy told me that sometimes, Pony's oldest daughter hung out here. When I got to the front door, I wasted no time ringing the bell while pulling my pistol out, and keeping it concealed behind my back. The sound of movement came immediately and a few seconds later, the door was pulled open. I'd seen a picture or two of Pony when he was younger, so it was easy to see the familiar relationship between the man I despised, and the one holding the door open.

"You're Pony's son, huh?" I asked.

"Who wants to know?"

The smartass reply came with just the right amount of cockiness and arrogance to put a smile on my face.

"The devil wants to know," I replied, swiftly pressing my gun to his forehead.

His eyes widened and his mouth opened, but he never got a word out before I pulled the trigger. I made sure to grab the front of his shirt before shooting him so that I could dictate which way his body dropped as I stepped into the house. I kicked the door closed behind me and let junior slump by the umbrella stand. The sound of screams made my head swing to the left where I came face to face with the child I'd *expected* to see. I raised my gun and took aim at her mouth, which suddenly shut her up.

"You didn't have to stop on my account sweetheart, quick question though, where's your grandma?"

" Up upstairs," she murmured.

"I appreciate that see ya around kid."

Her eyes widened in terror seconds before I pulled the trigger, and they went glassy in death. I quickly ran to the backdoor, let Demon in, and then made a beeline for the staircase. There were four rooms on the upper level of the house, but I easily found my target behind door number two. The sounds of her shower must've drowned out the commotion downstairs because she was still lathering up her flabby, pale skin with soap, and humming softly.

"Am I interrupting?" I asked casually.

The sound of my voice scared her so bad that her dentures went flying out of her mouth and skipped across the linoleum floor until they hit my feet.

"Ewwww, and more eww," I said, frowning down at her runaway furniture.

"Wh-what do you want? I don't have much money, but you can take it all, just please don't hurt us."

"Hurting you is the only reason I'm here. Sorry," I replied, shooting her point-blank in the chest.

When she collapsed onto the floor outside the shower, I stepped forward and fired two more shots into her face.

"You look cuter with dimples," I said, chuckling as I turned and left.

Demon was posted at the bottom of the steps waiting for me.

"Torch the house and meet me in the truck," I said, tucking my pistol as I headed out the front door.

When I got inside my truck, I took a deep breath and laid my head against the seat. The feeling in my chest couldn't be described as remorse for what I just did because I knew that I would do it again in a heartbeat. I was more upset because I promised myself that the old me was gone for good, and I'd convinced myself that I was better for it. The real truth was *she* made me a better man, and so for her, there was *nothing* I wouldn't do. If that damned me to hell, then I was okay with that because I knew my Gini would join me without hesitation.

The smell of smoke filled my nose just as Demon climbed into the seat next to me. I quickly started my engine and eased away from the curb at a normal rate of speed. We didn't appear to be more than partners out for an afternoon drive, and I felt secure behind my truck's dark tent.

"YoBruh, what was that all about back there?" Demon asked.

Just handling some business my nigga, and I appreciate you rolling with me."

"You know that I always gotcha back Bruh, no matter what," he replied sincerely.

"Yeah, I know. What I *don't know* is why you are still out here in these streets smoking that wet, especially since we talked about that. What's the rule?"

He didn't answer my question, he simply accepted his gaze out the passenger side windows. I wasn't questioning him to humiliate him, I was doing it because I was my brother's keeper and that came before anything. *almost!*

"What's the rule Demon?"

"The rule is money over everything."

"Right, so how much money do you have in your pockets?" I asked.

When he reached into his jeans and pulled a few crumpled one-dollar bills with a $10 dollar bill in the mix with some coins, I started to slap the shit out of him; the fact that he couldn't even look me in the eye told me that I didn't even have to go that far to prove my point though. I simply shook my head disgustedly, turned my music back up, and headed back the way we'd come. Almost 2 hours later, I pulled up at the same 7-11 in Alexandria that I'd picked him up from, and I stopped.

"Listen Bruh, I fuck with you, and you know that by now. You gotta show some improvement though. So, you've got exactly 30 days to bring $50,000 dollars or your seat at my table is gone. I don't support junkies bruh, I support the hustler, understand?" I asked.

"I gotcha," he mumbled, as he slid out of the truck.

Part of me always wanted to take something out of the hand of my man in the street, but a kingdom wasn't just made up of a King, it took soldiers of all kinds and I hadn't gotten too big-headed to remember that. As Demon walked across the parking lot from me, I pulled out my phone and shot a message to a female soldier of mine; within moments, I'd gotten the reply that I was looking for, and I pulled off back into traffic.

Two blunts and an hour later, I pulled up at a motel room not far from Richmond. I spotted Sarah's jeep immediately, and as soon as I'd parked beside it, the motel room door opened directly in front of me. I grabbed my phone and my weed and hopped out.

"This is a surprise, but L I'm not sure if it's a pleasant one or not," she said, looking at me curiously.

"That all depends on you slim."

She took a step back and allowed me into the dimly lit room. We'd never used this particular mote before, and I liked the fact that she's been really paying attention when I said never go to the same place twice. If we moved like we were always being watched, then we stood less of a chance of someone seeing more than we wanted them to see. I took a seat in the chair by the table, while she posted up on the bed with her back to the headboard.

"You working tonight?" I asked

"Yeah, gotta go in at 6 p.m."

"I want you to put in your two-week notice," I said.

For a moment, she didn't respond; she simply stared at me with her dark green eyes. The green was sexier than the blue contacts she wore to work, and they made her more believable natural blond.

"Why?" She asked.

"Because I said so and that should be enough of a reason."

My answer caused the diamond-studded nose ring in her nostril to flare, as she took her long hair out of its messy bun and put it back up. This was a nervous habit with her, as well as fidgeting when she was bored. Despite the fact that she's only 24-years-old, I'd known her for a while, and we'd only made it this far because I liked her more than her looks. We'd met during one of my stints in Haynesville Correctional when she was just a rookie Correctional Officer that most of us called Baby Barns.

Her mom had worked for the Department of Corrections too, which typically meant she was off limits because she should've been impervious to inmate charm. For the most part, she was, but I hadn't approached her like most niggas. I hadn't wanted what was in between her legs, I'd wanted what was in between her ears. To my way of thinking, what a cute young chick from Warsaw/Tappahannock Virginia didn't wanna make some *REAL* money without having to fuck and suck for it? So, I'd made her an offer she couldn't refuse, knowing in the back of my mind that all roads led to this moment right here. The end game.

"Look L, if this is about me ending your visit with Gini I'm sorry, but you know that I gotta make it look good for everyone watching."

"I know that, and I completely understand, but this ain't about that."

"Then why-ooooh shit," she mumbled.

I could tell by the light in her eyes that she finally understood my request.

"Are you really crazy enough to break her out? I mean you *do* understand that you would have to run *forever*, right?" she asked.

"I'm aware."

"Damn... I gotta ask her what tricks she knows because you're about to go *all in* for the pussy." she said, laughing

"Gini and I have never done more than kiss. It's deeper than the physical."

She kept laughing until she realized I wasn't bullshitting her in the slightest.

"You really never- not even before she got locked up?"

"No Sarah, we've really *never* had sex."

"Oh wow! So, it's love, like *real love* that's making you do all of this that you've been doing and are about to do", she said, in awe.

"It's that and...and so much more than I can put into words."

The look in her eyes became a beautiful kaleidoscope of wonder, admiration, and envy, with respect underlying all things.

"You know I used to wonder why you never tried to seduce me, but now I think I understand and I'm relieved that you don't think something is wrong with me," she said sincerely.

"There's absolutely nothing wrong with you slim, you're a beautiful girl. I just couldn't have you going in there looking her in the face every day if you and I had fucked because that would've caused all kinds of problems."

"Damn L, you talking like your dick would've put a neon sign on my forehead or something."

We both laughed at the image she painted. But I quickly steered the conversation back to the business at hand.

"I need you to put in your notice, but we'll be long gone before that day comes", I said.

"I don't wanna know what day you're planning this shit for, but will you need me to do anything special?"

"Make this the last delivery of drugs to her tonight and tell her to be ready to throw the biggest party that prison has ever seen," I replied.

"I got you."

In the normal weekly package, I send Gini weed, suboxone, and Percocet, but I'd changed up in the last two weeks in preparation for my next move. Instead of sending Perc 30's, I'd had fentanyl pressed into pill form with nobody being the wiser. Normally, it takes 21 days to form any habit, but that Fen-Fen was a different animal altogether, and since I was a few days late with the pack, I knew their bodies were calling to them like zombies needing brains to feed on. Human beings in general barely knew what moderation meant, so it was no secret as to why a junkie would sell their soul. This was just my way of buying a few.

"Ima give you $10,000 for this last run so that after the smoke clears, you won't be pressed to go back to work. You can if you want to, but you don't have to", I said.

"Thanks L... Can I ask you for a favor on top of that?"

"It depends on what it is", I replied.

Again, she got quiet, her nostrils flared, and then she took her hair down. Only this time she didn't put it back up into a messy bun, she just let the blond strands frame her face and roll just past her shoulders.

"I won't see you again after she's out huh?"

"You probably won't see me again after today," I said honestly.

"Well, if that's the case then...."

She let her words trail off as she slowly got up off the bed and moved towards me. She pointed at the weed, and I passed it to her, not understanding if that was the favor she was speaking of. Once she had a blunt out and lit, she tossed the rest on the table next to me, while pacing in a tiny line invisible to everyone except her. When she passed me the blunt, I took it and hit it, but I almost choked immediately because of her next move.

Without a word, she stopped in front of me and swiftly pulled her t-shirt over her head. My eyes immediately went to the baby blue laced material covering her modest-sized breasts, and my mind went to the next logical question. Did the panties match? As if she could read my mind, her jeans suddenly hit the floor, and the baby blue lace was now at my eye level. The scent of peaches filled my nostrils, dominating the good Kush mingling in the air and causing me to finally meet her unwavering gaze.

"I've never been with a black man L."

Chapter 8
October 2022
(3 Months later)

"I *hate* you."

"I hate you too baby." I growled thru clenched teeth while trying to cum quietly.

Having phone sex with niggas on the phones on either side of me was bold even for my crazy ass, but Gini was just as adventurous as I was, so we indulged whenever the mood hit. For us, that was daily, but neither of us complained.

"L!"

The way she said my name told me that at that very moment, her sweet pussy juices were gushing over her fingers, and that made me smile.

"Do you still hate me, baby?" I asked smiling.

"Yes, but only because I love your big black ass."

"And I love you my little wop", I said chuckling, while wiping my own cum on my boxer shorts.

If you asked either of us, neither of us could explain how we'd gotten to this point of no return that we were currently living in. Just a short three months ago I'd been kicking it with Angela, and Gini had been kicking it with a nigga named Catfish, but we'd said *fuck them* and chosen each other somehow. I'd never known a woman more fascinating, and versatile before because she was smart enough to keep up with my ADHD moments when I jumped conversations like a leapfrog. A conversation might start with a '67 Chevelle, change gears to prison cuisine, hang a left at why her ass was bigger than most black women, and speed right into the NBA season! We literally talked about *EV-ER-Y-THING* while still managing to flirt enough to require two climaxes worth of phone sex. I never considered myself to have a dream girl type, but Gini had proved me wrong in more ways than one.

"L, you're gonna forget about me."

"How can you say that babe? I just told your crazy ass that you're my WOP!" I stated emphatically.

"Yeah, I know, but there's other bitches out there who'll be throwing pussy at you like confetti."

"I can't compete with that."

"You got it wrong baby, it's *them* that can't compete with *YOU*! I keep telling you that sex ain't better than love, so no matter what it's always gonna be you and I," I vowed.

Her silence spoke loudly to the insecurity she was obviously feeling, but I didn't mind taking the time to walk her through the landmines of her emotions. If I had as much time as she did, I would find it hard to believe my damn self that somebody actually wanted to hold me down. I planned to show her that I was a different type of nigga though, just like she was a rare type of woman. Together, we were made for each other though.

"Did you call my sister Micaela and let her know that your appeal was granted, and your release has been approved?" She asked.

"I tried to call, but you know that her ass ain't never in the house, especially when her grandson Mason is down there playing with his dog Max."

"Yeah, I know, it's just that I want you to go meet everybody before you get too busy." She explained

"Baby, I'll *never* be too busy for my in-laws. Tell me what's really bothering you, Virginia."

I know that my use of her full name would let her know how serious I was, even though I wasn't mad at her. I loved her, and I, therefore, did my best to be patient.

"I just don't wanna lose you Leroy, and I'm really scared because I love you like I've never loved anyone. Not even Pony made me feel the way you do."

Her heartfelt confession made me smile and feel warm all over, but it was bittersweet because the pain of leaving her caged in went to my soul.

"You big pussy! You know I'm not leaving you babe, and you know why", I said.

"Why?"

"Because I love you in the exact same way, and I'm gonna marry you", I replied,

"M-marry me? What?"

Her confusion over this simple yet important concept made me laugh. I could picture the blank stare on her beautiful face, but she was too smooth to panic.

"Why are you so surprised babe? Marriage is the natural step in any relationship that has progressed far enough", I said logically

"Yeah, I get that you asshole, but *US* getting married? I just didn't think you'd want to."

"Gini, we talked about marriage when we first got together, and I *TOLD YOU* that I wanted to get married again someday. Now, I'm telling you that the only way to do it is if you're my wife."

She got quiet for a few moments, but I could still hear other females in the background, so I knew she was still on the phone.

"Marriage? Well, ok. I *do* love your ass, but you just better make sure that every bitch out in them streets *knows* who has your heart L. I'm dead ass serious about that. Oh, and I wanna talk to these sister-wife bitches that are tryna trap you too."

"No problem, babe, I'll set that call up tonight", I replied, smiling widely.

"Good, now fight with me so that I can cum one more time before the phone hangs up."

"You know I like it when you're demanding", I say, already sliding my hand back into my boxers.

With time being of the essence, it was a short 7 minutes later when we came together for the second time. I got off the phone and headed straight to the bathroom to clean myself up so that I could officially start my day.

"Ayo L, who's getting your TV?" Red asked.

"Buckshot is getting everything I got bruh, so holla at him."

Thankfully, Red took this answer and stepped off because I was so tired of this question that I wanted to scream loudly. I didn't do that though, I just got myself together and headed for my bed area. Most niggas were still asleep, and I was good with that because a whole lot of fake goodbyes weren't my thing. Not even my family knew I was getting out, except for Byrd, because being invisible was my new mo. This trip back into the pos of hell had taught me that everything happens for a reason, and now I was walking with a different purpose. I used my almost four months of incarceration wisely, so now I was posed to step out of prison as a legitimate businessman.

"Yo L, Duke is looking for you."

I didn't see who had relayed this message, but it didn't matter because I'd meant to go holla at my dawg anyway. I came out of the bathroom and headed for the front door so that I could step out into the entryway. Before the door even opened, I spotted my nigga sitting in one corner of the entry, grinning from ear to ear. Once I stepped out, he rose to his full 5'9 and threw his 240lbs at me in a brotherly hug.

"Damn, I wish I was going with you bro."

"Come on my nigga, you already know that you're with me 100% of the way and that's set-in-stone," I replied sincerely.

"I appreciate that bro because a lot of niggas be faking once they get out, but I know you definitely bout the shit we've been talking about."

"Absolutely, and I appreciate you giving me the game. I gotcha for life Bruh," I vowed.

"That's what I know, listen though, I'ma hit you up in a few days just to make sure that you got both feet on the ground. Remember to take your time and keep all fuck shit from around you."

"Duke you know that I ain't no dummy, so trust me when I tell you that I'ma be all the way on my square out there. Just call me whenever you need to."

We dapped each other up, and then he got the C/O in the booth to buzz him thru back to his side. I went back in my pod and headed to my bed area to finish packing the little bit of shit that I was taking with me. With that out of the way, I made one last call and then checked my email. At 8:45 a.m. I was paged to the front of the unit, and I knew that it was really and truly over.

I said goodbye to the niggas I considered family while smiling in the face of the extreme hate from the hoe niggas that couldn't stand my black ass. By 9:05 a.m. I was stepping outside into the bright morning sunshine moving with purpose to the back door of the Lincoln Town car limo waiting for me.

"Welcome home Mr. Bly. Everything that you requested is waiting on you in the car," the driver said, opening the door for me.

"Thanks, let's go," I said, sliding onto the cool leather seat.

Once the door was closed, it took a moment for my eyes to adjust to the neon orange lighting glow from the bar.

"I gotta hand it to you Mr. Bly, you sure do know how to make a girl feel special."

Hearing her voice made my eyes adjust quicker because I suddenly saw her long-legged silhouette sitting almost directly behind the driver's seat.

"I told you Luna, I got you," I said.

She moved closer to me once the car pulled off while lighting a blunt that instantly had the Car smelling like Blueberries.

"Well, now that you have me Leroy, what is it that you plan to do?"

"That really depends on you sweetheart, honestly. You know that you're way too smart to be working for the Department of Corrections, and you're too honest to go dirty to make the extra money. So, in my mind, that only leaves one option, which is that we go into business together," I concluded.

"Doing what exactly?" she asked, passing me the blunt.

I hit it mightily and held it in until the smoke was forced to trickle from my nose. I didn't know If it was because I'd been locked up or if my tolerance was way low. Either way, I was feeling like I was walking on air.

"You come from Seattle which more or less makes you a West Coaster, and to me, that signifies some knowledge of Marijuana and how it grows. It's a known fact that Seattle is like the rain capital of the USA, which means you'll be good at growing in any weather. So, what I want is a field of good weed, using a greenhouse and natural outdoor growing procedures too."

"Wait, so you want me to be the manufacture, or you want me to oversee the operation?" she asked.

"Both. I want you to know everything that you can about the cannabis business, and both I and my sister will learn the same things. That's how you make one grow operation a franchise," I replied, passing her the blunt back.

She smoked quietly, obviously contemplating the proposition I'd made. From my first conversation with Luna, I'd known that she was more than a Correction Officer with a pretty face, and that was the onset of the plan that I'd just laid out for her.

Neither of us was the type to judge the other, and we could both understand the benefits of continuing a friendship once I was out. The only question now was how far could we take it.

"So, would I be working for you or with you?"

"Both, actually because I don't simply wanna put you on salary for all that you'll be required to do. I wanna give you a percentage of the company we're about to form while it's still in its beginning stages. To me, that makes this shit bigger than business, and it makes you part of the family. You know how loyal I am," I replied, reaching for the bottle of Patron 1800 in the bar.

"You better be careful with that."

When I looked over at her, she was smiling wickedly, and she gave a slight nod to the bottle in my hand. I started to reply that I'd only been gone for four months, but I took into consideration how high a couple of hits of good green had one right now. When I popped the top on the bottle, I took a small swig before slapping the cap back on and putting it away.

"I must admit L, your proposition sounds very intriguing."

"But?" I prompted.

"But mixing business with pleasure *NEVER* turns out right," she replied, again passing me the blunt.

I felt the wave of confusion roll through my brain for a second, and I hit the blunt in an effort to clear my head.

"You and I have never mixed any business with personal, so I don't see the problem."

Her response came in the form of her moving to the seat beside me and staring deeply into my eyes. I waited for her to speak, but her communication was non-verbal because her hand slithered into my state-issued Khaki pants swiftly. My dick was hard before she could grab it for real, but the aggressive way she grabbed it pushed the smoke from my lungs and made my dick harder.

"You better stop playing," I warned.

"Who's playing Leroy?"

She pulled my dick free before I could respond while sliding to her knees in between my legs. I put the blunt in the ashtray just as she wrapped her lips around the head of my dick and sucked forcefully enough to render me breathless. My eyes rolled, my mind scrambled, and the ringing in my ears sounded like freedom.

Chapter 9
2027

Shy wasn't a word that anyone would ever use to describe me. At least, not if they knew me, but the move Sarah had just pulled had me speechless. I was far from being scared of pussy, but I was smart enough to fear the consequences of fucking the wrong female. I opened my mouth to say just that when the sound of my phone ringing cut through the sexual tension like a chainsaw.

I quickly pulled my phone out, and once I saw who was calling, I mouthed the words 'Rain Check' while making my exit. I grabbed my weed and stuffed it in my pocket as I answered the phone by telling the person on the other end to hold on. Once I made it back to my truck and pulled off I spoke freely.

"What's up Charlene?"

"Nothing, I was just wondering if you were busy right now."

"Are you okay?" I asked, sensing something in her tone.

"Yeah, I guess."

I'd heard the hesitation in her voice, so I knew instantly that she wasn't giving me the entire truth.

"I'm on my way, just tell me where you are," I replied.

"I'm at home. Alone."

I didn't say anything else, I simply hung up and headed in her direction. When I'd met Charlene, our relationship was just supposed to be about business because she was a nurse inside Fluvanna Correctional Center. She was the one nurse who'd always taken care of Gini, and so Gini had asked me to look out for her. The first time I'd seen the 5'1 ¾, 150lbs, brown-haired beauty, I thought it was an obvious test by my wife.

Charlene had a beauty that radiated from her gorgeous smile up to her breathtaking greenish-brown eyes, but she was humble about it. She wasn't the type to let her beauty go to her head, and that only made her sexier in my eyes. Normally, she was the type of woman I'd approach, but she was married and so was I, which pushed us into the comfort of the friend zone. I was good with that though because she was cool as shit to be around.

Her husband was a different story altogether. It was beyond me to understand how any *sane man* could take a good woman for granted, but Charlene's husband definitely didn't appreciate her. It took me just under an hour to get to her spot, and soon as she opened the door, I could tell she'd been crying. She stepped into my open arms and rested her head on my heart.

I stepped inside with her and closed the door so that her nosey neighbors wouldn't have the privilege of witnessing her vulnerability. No words we exchanged, but the quivering in her body told me that she was once again crying. I let her have all the time that she needed, and once she pulled it together, she took a small step back from me. When I looked down, I saw that her eyes were more grey than green or brown, which was a testament to her sadness. I saw past that though because her sex appeal was undeniable.

"What happened Charlene?"

"Nothing in particular, I just-I just don't feel the love that I need. I mean I know that I work a lot, but when I'm not working, I definitely try to focus on our relationship. I'm not perfect L, but I'm a *good woman*," she stated passionately.

"You *ARE* a good woman sweetheart, and you can never let what he does make you doubt that."

She nodded her head, but I could tell that her heart wasn't in it for real. I let my instincts take over then, and I leaned in until my lips touched hers. The shock she felt was like an electrical current that flowed from her to me, but it didn't make her pull back. My tongue made her lips part at the same time that her hands pulled me towards her swiftly. Her mouth held the sweetness of grapes mixed with tears, and the taste of pure unchecked hunger too.

When she pushed my shirt up over my head, I followed her lead and started undressing her. Within seconds we were down to just underwear and heated flesh, and our kisses were so full of fire that they were sucking the oxygen out of the air around us. That only left opportunity standing in between her and I. Our kiss was broken long enough for me to check her eyes for consent without the complications of regret. Once I saw that, I quickly spun her around until her back and juicy ass were pressed against the hardness fighting for attention through my boxer briefs.

Taking her hands, I laced our fingers together while maneuvering her towards the closest wall so that she could assume the position.

"Don't move, just hold on," I instructed huskily.

My hands stayed on hers as I kissed down the back of her neck, and across her shoulder blades. The rhythm of her breathing was shaky, but the desire was palpable, and it was my source of inspiration. With a practiced move of skill, I used one hand to swiftly unhook her bra and released her breasts along with her gasp of surprise. I spun her back towards me and put her back against the wall while my lips explored the hollow in her throat.

My kisses had her attention so that by the time my tongue flicked across her nipples, her hands had found their way to my dreadlocks. She held on tight under the intense pressure my tongue was applying, but I knew just how to break her. I kneeled in front of her, pulling her panties down on my way so that she could step out of them. With my hands on her thick thighs, I forced her to take a small step to open her legs, while licking from her navel down to her beautifully trimmed love triangle.

My tongue struck out at her clit with a snake-like vengeance, causing her body to tremble beneath my touch. Her pussy smelled like fresh rain, and I didn't hesitate to take a taste of her.

"L!" she gasped, grabbing my hair tighter.

I ignored the plea that was unmistakable in her voice while diving fast into her deliciousness. Just me licking in between her pussy lips and sucking on her clit had her moaning at a feverish pitch, but when I introduced two of my fingers to her vaginal walls, her moans became chants.

"Oh-Oh-Oh," she stammered, grinding against my tongue and hand simultaneously.

The pressure of her orgasm was building faster than a tornado in Oklahoma, and she was too helpless to stop it. I ate her pussy until I felt like I could peek inside her and see her climax rolling through her. Without warning, I stood up and picked her up so that I could carry her into the bedroom she shared with her husband. After laying her down on top of the plush white comforter, I stepped back, and slowly pushed my boxers down over my hips.

By the time they hit the floor, she was staring at my dick with unashamed need. She spread her legs wide enough for me to see the pussy juices already drizzling down towards the crack of her ass. I stepped out of my last piece of clothing and stepped into my first stroke by climbing on top of her and pushing my dick deep inside her. The way her legs clapped closed around my waist brought about a mental picture of being caught in a bear trap.

Her honey had me stuck but moving with speed and power as I gave her that good love she'd been missing. It only took a handful of thorough strokes before the gushing began, and her pussy tried to drown me.

"Le-Roy!" she cried out, clutching me tightly.

I fucked her harder in the face of her hurricane, and I was rewarded with a freak storm in the form of a mini climax directly following her first one. Her pussy grip tightened, but I fought my own climax by switching up the position. We separated long enough for me to flip her on her side and push her right leg at just the right angle for me to slide right back inside her. I made sure to rub her clit while pounding her pussy steadily.

"Oh-Oh L! wait-wait a minute."

At first, I thought that she was simply caught up in the throws of passion, but I saw fear when she looked over at me. It was on the tip of my tongue to ask her what was wrong, but then I heard a noise that was out of place.

"I got you," I said, slamming my dick back inside her faster and harder.

She quickly clamped her hands over her own mouth to suppress the screams clawing at her windpipe, but the sound of the headboard slapping echoed like gunshots. I couldn't hear the garage door opening anymore, which meant her husband was more than likely in the garage, and seconds away from walking in on us. The thought of us getting caught made my looming journey of fulfillment that much sweeter, and moments later, I happily filled Charlene with my cum.

Once my dick stopped jumping, I pulled out of her and hopped up at a dead run for the front door. The fact that my dick was still dripping with her pussy juices and cum didn't faze me in the slightest because I was only focused on getting to my pile of clothes. I managed to reach my destination seconds before I heard a door open and the sounds of heavy boots assaulting the linoleum floor. I knew that I didn't have time to get dressed, so I simply grabbed my gun, and spun towards the direction that her husband would enter from.

"Charlene, why don't I smell my dinner? Where the hell are you woman, and-."

His questions and obvious irritation froze in the same instant that he saw me standing there with my gun outstretched in front of me. His eyes suddenly dropped to my dick which made me feel hella weird, and when he looked back up at me, there was clear understanding swimming across his iris.

"Who the fuck are you?" he growled at me, clenching his big meaty fists.

Charlene picked that exact moment to enter the room, sauntering in a way that made her nakedness irresistible to any man.

"You're home early honey, and that's why your dinner ain't ready. Plus, I was getting a much-needed fucking," she said, crossing the room to stand beside me.

"Wh-what?" he croaked.

"Fucked sweetheart, as in this nice-sized black dick attached to him was deep inside me, and I mean deep inside me," she bragged, gesturing towards my manhood like she was Vanna White's stand-in on 'Wheel of Fortune'.

Despite how serious this situation was, I couldn't help chuckling because of the expression on the man's face in front of me. The shock was clearly warring with the rage, but I had no illusions about which one was gonna win in the end.

"I'll tell you what Greg, if you leave for like an hour or so, so that I can finish getting thoroughly dicked down, then

I'll cook you the best meal you've ever had. Is that a good deal?" she asked.

The way his mouth opened and closed made him look like a combination of a big baby and a hungry fish. Not a word was uttered from him though. Finally, Charlene sighed in frustration and stepped in front of me.

"Fine, I guess you wanna watch," she said, dropping to her knees in front of me.

I never got the chance to stop her before she took my dick fully into her mouth and began sucking me like a good Slurpee. My vision blurred, but not so hard as to prevent me from seeing him lunge at us. My first shot barely slowed his progress, which forced me from aiming at his chest to his face and squeezing off two more shots. He dropped and slid to a stop right next to us, but not even that stopped her from eating her treat.

She caught a fast-paced rhythm and a few minutes later, I could barely hold my gun as my knees trembled like an earthquake was trapped in my body. When my cum exploded to the back of her mouth she didn't gag, she just gargled and swallowed every drop.

"You-you're something else," I stammered, looking down into her upturned face.

"I'm glad that you recognize that L because I know that you can appreciate me. All of me."

I made sure to pull my dick all the way away from her before verbalizing my thoughts.

"Exactly what is it that you're expecting from me?" I asked slowly, not relaxing my grip on my pistol.

"I just expect you to treat me like you always have, and not let the sex change things between us."

I looked at her and looked at the dead man mere inches from us both. Things had *definitely* changed after we'd had sex and those changes were irreversible.

"I got you, but you gotta do something for me," I stated.

The smile she gave me made my heart beat faster, but I was far from scared.

"Whatever you want."

Chapter 10
2022
(7 days later)

"Everything I give you is brand new out of the box, no bodies, and not reported stolen. For that, you gotta pay the price I set."

I continued my thorough inspection of the Draco in my hand while my mind thought through my plans. Given everything that I'd been through, I knew that logically, there should be *no way* I was holding another gun, but my protection would forever be my problem. My sister still didn't understand that, which is why she'd gotten rid of my pistol as soon as I'd gotten arrested. No matter the risk I faced at getting caught with a gun, the reality was that the takeover required weapons.

"How many can I get?" I asked, looking up at my nigga, IG.

"You can get whatever you want as long as you got the money for it."

IG was an infinite Gangster, hence the nickname, but he was also a hustla and a businessman. Our ties dated back to when we were both trapped behind enemy lines and razor wire, forced to be students of the law like we were students of the game once upon a time. Real had recognized real, and the rest was history, which was why I'd called him up after I realized that I needed to go all in on my artillery. All it took was a few seconds on the phone and two days later, the 6'1, 210lbs gravely voice killer showed up at my apartment with a suitcase full of fun.

"Come on my nigga, you know that my money is as straight as your mohawk," I replied.

He chuckled while running his hand over his hair in question.

"So, tell me what you need L-Boogie."

"Give me two Glock .17's with 30 rounds each, two Draco's, an AK-47 and a SIG .45," I said seriously.

He turned to his mobile office and began pulling the requested items out and sat them on my couch. If my neighbors knew what I was up to, they would probably have the Prince Williams Police Department out in full force to stop me. Niggas and bitches in Woodbridge, VA wasn't pussy, they were just shaky about people who weren't from out here carrying heavy firepower.

"I'ma throw in a few of these just because you my nigga and because you can never have too many grenades," he said sitting everything on my living room coffee table.

I sat down and began a thorough inspection of each weapon. It didn't take more than a curious glance before I looked him in the eyes and gave him the nod of approval before I got up off the couch and headed to my back bedroom. I made sure to move to my floor safe quietly so that I didn't wake Luna up. I grabbed a stack of hundred-dollar bills, knowing that this particular bundle was $5k and returned to the living room.

"Keep the change," I said, tossing IG the money.

"Of course, I will," he replied, laughing as he pocketed the cash and began packing his stuff up.

I took all of my guns and returned to my safe to store them while we conducted the rest of our business. By the time I got back to the living room Zuk was sitting on the couch next to IG, and they were talking amongst themselves. Together, they'd founded the nation of rulers bike club and forever change the way America view black businessmen. IG was the national president of the club and Zuk was the VP of the nation, but they moved like there were no big I's and little U's.

The overall goal of world domination was more important than any title either man carried, and I respected that about them. The fact that Zuk was 5'9, 186lbs., with brown skin and humble, often made people underestimate the magnitude of his violence, but it was a lesson that most muthafuckas learned quickly. These weren't young kittens I was dealing with. IG was 50 and Zuk was 52, which made them seasoned lions in any jungle they stepped into, but the bloodstains on their teeth were always fresh.

"What's up Zuk?" I said, sitting across from both men on my white leather love seat.

"Same ole, same ole. It's good to see you back out, so just make sure you don't go back in for any reason," he replied.

"We've got some serious business on the horizon and we're talking about the kind of money that rewrites history," IG stated.

"I'm here for it. What's up?" I asked, curiously.

"There's about to be a new wave warcot that's blankets the world, and we have the opportunity to be the first ones in the water," Zuk replied.

"What's the drug and what does it do?" I asked.

"It makes Fentanyl look like you're trying to get high on aspirin, but it doesn't have the same mortality rate when it comes to overdosing. We call it Future," IG replied.

I knew the power of Fen-Fen without having dabbled with it because I'd lost some good men to it, so to hear them talk about how mild it was compared to this new drug called Future made me nervous. One thing that I knew for sure was that this could be like getting in on the ground floor of

Amazon and no amount of nerves would make me miss that opportunity.

"Tell me what the plan is," I said, giving my full attention.

"Well, this drug gives you everything you could want without the side effects. You can fuck your bitch all night long without going soft and if she takes it, then that pussy will; never go dry. At the same time, you retain the focus necessary to escape the bag and bust a nigga in the head if needed," Zuk replied.

"Damn, that shit does sound like everything a muthafucka would want! What's in it?" I asked, scooting to the edge of my seat.

"The recipe is a closely guarded secret, so listen closely and don't write anything down," IG replied seriously.

We spent the next hour huddled together, plotting and planning until Luna walked into the room wearing only my t-shirt and rubbing the sleep from her eyes.

"We got some business to handle but we'll meet up again soon," IG said, standing up and grabbing the handle of his rolling suitcase.

Zuk followed his lead, and they made their exit as quickly as they'd come.

"I didn't mean to interrupt L, I was just wondering where you'd gone."

I gave her my best seductive smile while moving toward her and taking her into my arms.

"You're used to me waking you up with the dick already, huh?"   I asked.

She blushed beautifully, but still nodded her head without shame. When I leaned in to kiss her, I slowly pulled the t-shirt over her head, until she was naked in my arms. With my hands on her hips, I backed up to the loveseat and sat down so that she could straddle me. She wasted no time taking her position, while simultaneously pulling out my dick and easing down onto it.

The way we joined together was poetry in motion and it only intensified when her mouth met mine again for more exchanging of fire. I was so lost in her slow and patient rhythm that I didn't realize we weren't alone until the sounds of someone clearing their throat echoed loudly throughout my living room. Our lips separated and we both looked towards the front door.

"Meet me in your bedroom," Byrd said, shaking her head as she walked up the hallway.

As badly as I wanted to travel deeper into the Candyland of Luna's good pussy, I knew that the look in my sister's eyes was strictly business.

"Go make breakfast," I said lifting her off me.

"How about I order it and say it's homemade?"

"That's fine, just stay out here until I come back," I replied, pulling cash out of my pocket and handing it to her.

With that handled, I straightened my appearance and headed for my room. When I got there, I found my sister rolling a blunt with the speed and efficiency of a money machine, still wearing an annoyed expression. I closed the door behind me and braced for impact.

"What's goody, sis?"

"Have you done more than stick your dick in that white girl since you been out my nigga?" she asked, without looking at me.

It was on the tip of my tongue to respond with some smart-ass shit about fucking my daughter Lia's mom, but I knew better than to poke this particular bear.

"I've been handling business too, you know that."

"Okay, but there are things more important than money or pussy bruh, and you should be mature enough to know that shit. Have you even *attempted* to reach out to Cyn?" she asked, finally looking up at me.

"I tried but she's not speaking to me., she ain't has shit to say since she sent me that letter blaming me for her mother's death."

"L, she's *hurting,* and that shit is eating her up inside, I follow her on Snapchat and Instagram and I'm here to tell you that your daughter has stepped into the streets with both feet! She's selling dope a mile a minute and from what I hear, she's toting a pistol too."

"Who the fuck gave my daughter dop and a gun?" I asked, instantly furious.

"I don't know all that, but bruh she needs you. She's fucking with some lil nigga named Rome who's in the street, so my best guess is that's who's playing Clyde to her Bonnie. You remember what it was like to be her age and feel like all you had was the one person that loved you without judgement? You and Mercedes had that type of love, and nobody could tell you shut."

The truth of her words suddenly threw me into the past and with every memory came a feeling of anxiety about the path my daughter was travelling. I wanted her to be better than me, and I felt like her mom would want the same thing.

"Has Lia said anything to her?" I asked.

"I mean, she tried, but that's not her job it's yours."

I was used to my sister giving me uncut dope when it came to the truth, but it still didn't make it any easier to hear. We were silent for a few moments and then she passed me a lit blunt as a peace offering. I hit it hard while contemplating my next move. I didn't doubt Byrd's accounting of what was going on which told me everything probably started and stopped with the lil nigga Rome that Cyn was dating. If I removed him, then the chess board would be restructured, and the young Queen could be saved before she sacrificed herself unnecessarily.

"I'll take care of it sis," I vowed.

"Make sure that happens sooner than later because you know that death is permanent my nigga."

I nodded my head in understanding before passing her the blunt back. We ended up smoking two blunts while I filled her in on my immediate business plans, and then she left to go have lunch with her dude. I spent a few moments in my room in reflective silence just trying to plot out my move concerning my daughter.

"Baby, you hungry?" Luna asked, coming in the room with a Jimmy John's sub in her hand.

"I'll eat it later, but we need to talk really quick, so come sit next to me."

She did as I instructed while trying not to look as nervous as the words 'WE need to talk' made most people.

"I need you to start working on the growing business, so I'ma get you a flight out west today. I want you to stay for a couple of weeks; find out all you can and then we'll go from there," I said.

She stared at me hard for a minute and I could read the questions that crossed her mind as if she'd spoken out loud.

"No, you haven't done anything wrong, and no this ain't the end of us."

"Okay, so that means that you're sending me out of town because you're about to do something that you shouldn't," she stated.

I didn't say anything in response to her theory, which kinda said it all.

"I can help you Leroy."

"I know you can and that's why I need you to get on a plane and fly to Cali today," I replied.

She nodded slowly before sitting my food on the bed and walking to the bathroom. After she closed the door, I heard the shower come on. I knew that I had to make this a smoother exit than this, but my first order of business was to hit Lia up and tell her to find out everything she could about Cyn's boyfriend. While she handled that, I went to my safe to get one of the Glock .17's with the 30-round clip and I combined the two before tossing the gun on my bed.

I walked into the bathroom, stripped and stepped into the shower with Luna. As soon as our eyes met, she knew the bell for round one had been rung. It was time to fuck like we might never do it again because this might just be our last chance.

Chapter 11
2027
(4 days later)

"Will You be back for dinner?" Candice asked, following me out of the house into the garage.

I wanted to just ignore her because she was annoying the fuck out of me, but instead, I took a deep breath and kept moving towards my bike in the corner. Something about seeing the custom paint job that was a combination of greens and blacks mixed with glittery diamonds falling calmed me. The Emerald green lettering that spelled out 'MONEY MACHINE' down the side only made the picture of Scrooge McDuck diving into a pile of gold pop out more. My 2026 Suzuki GSX-R 1100 was worthy of a supreme ruler, and I knew heads turned when I was on this bad muthafucka.

"Leroy?" Candice called out.

I stopped in front of my bike and turned to face her.

"For the last time Candice, I'm going underground in preparation for what we're about to do. I can't explain everything to you, and I don't know when I'll be back, but I'll on touch with you and Amelia until the curtain goes up. Okay?"

I could see the tears in her eyes, and I knew deep down in my soul that if she didn't pull it together, I was gonna shoot her muthafuckin ass. I didn't give her time to force my hand though, I just put my helmet on and climbed on my bike. I made sure to crank the engine so that I wouldn't have to hear her pleas, and then I gunned it. The squeal of tires echoed loudly as my bike shot out into the night only increasing my feeling of a dog breaking his leash.

Candice and Amelia weren't bad women, but they'd served their purpose and now it was time for me to move on from them. I had no doubts that they would be fine because I'd left them enough money for them to never have to work again, and I would tell them where it was once my disappearing act was complete. For now, my focus was on what would transpire within the next 48 hours. I pointed my bike in the direction of my new mistresses' house and open the throttle up until it felt like I was flying. Less than an hour later, I was pulling up outside Charlene's new temporary home in the city of Henrico, VA.

After I'd made her husband's body disappear, I'd had her rent a new spot in a gated community so that the people who knew her couldn't be in our business. For now, her husband's disappearance had gone unnoticed, but I knew that wouldn't last indefinitely. I parked my bike next to my Camaro in front of one side of the two-car garage and then I headed into the house. As soon as the door opened, the delicious smells of good food wafted out to greet me, and I tracked them to the huge kitchen at the back of the house. What I found when I got there brought my feet to a standstill and all I could do was observe. Charlene immediately felt my presence and glanced over her shoulder with a breathtaking smile on her face.

"Welcome home babe, I hope you're hungry."

"The food smells amazing...but the fact that you're standing there naked has my other appetite demanding more attention," I said seriously.

Her smile only got wider as she moved around the kitchen, but I could see the bluish-green tint to her eyes that indicated her ever-changing sexual mood.

"You'll get all of that in due time my King, but for now, let's start with a little Manicotti drizzled with my grandma's red sauce..."

"Sounds like a plan. Where are we eating?" I asked distractedly, while my eyes got full on every inch of her tanned, taut flesh.

"We can eat right here in the kitchen, just have a seat on one of the bar stools at the island."

I followed her order and pulled up a seat where I could observe her working. Charlene was a damn good nurse, but she was a better cook, and she took prize in her Italian/Scandinavian heritage. She didn't understand that this was like foreplay for me though, but I was only too eager to teach her these lessons. I didn't notice the phone sitting on the faux marble countertop beside me until it started ringing.

"That's for you," she called over her shoulder.

For a few seconds, I just stared at the phone like it was a new invention, but I finally grabbed it and hit the talk button.

"Hello?"

"Hey baby!" Gini said excitedly.

"What the fuck?" I said, unable to make my surprise at not hearing the automated voice of the prison recording before her voice.

"Why are you acting surprised like you didn't ask Charlene to bring me the same phone that you got?"

My eyes immediately shot to Charlene, and she was staring right back at me with a smile on her face wide enough to expose her sexy dimples.

"I mean I'm just surprised that you're calling right now," I replied.

"Well, I was told when you might show up to have dinner with Charlene and her husband, and I really wanted to talk to you. Listen L, I'm sorry about the other day and for not calling for the last few days. I just needed some time to wrap my head around what the lawyer had told me."

"I understand baby, and you don't have to apologize for anything. No matter what, you'll be in my arms soon. I promise," I stated passionately.

"I believe you baby, and I can't wait. Now tell me what you're having for dinner. Matter of fact, just put me on the speakerphone and let me ask the cook."

I hesitated for half a second, but I still did what she told me.

"Charlene are you there?" Gini asked.

"I'm here, just putting the finishing touches on the Manicotti."

"Are you having garlic bread with it?" Gini asked excitedly.

"Of course, we are with a nice full-bodied red wine to wash it down," Charlene replied.

"L, I hate you right now because you're about to eat *GOOD*! Plus, I know the weed you'll smoke afterward combined with the red wine is gonna have you ready to destroy my sister wives in the *BEDROOM*!"

Charlene's immediate laughter mixed seamlessly with Gini's, but I was too busy blushing to join them. I hadn't known exactly how much Gini had told Charlene about our relationship, but I saw no surprise in Charlene's eyes at the mention of me fucking with multiple women. Now, it made sense to me why she'd had no problems making our relationship physical for the first time the other day.

" Baby, you don't gotta hate me for the second part because I'm not going back to the house. I've got big business to handle," I said.

"Big business?" she echoed.

I could hear the immediate shift in her voice, which told me that she was paying attention.

"Yeah! Big business, which means I'm completely focused on everything except for pussy."

"Oh really?" Charlene asked.

When I looked over at her she was bending over touching her toes and smiling at me in between her opened legs. Her pussy was so pretty that I was speechless for a moment.

"L, are you there?" Gini asked.

"Uh, huh. I'm just looking at the meal I'm about to eat." I replied.

"Babe, you're a fat boy," Gini said laughing.

I was listening to my wife, but I was internally struggling with the question of why I hadn't told her that I was fucking Charlene because Gini and I didn't have secrets. The forbidden was always sexy, but when you loved someone, it was a weight to carry. Deep down I knew that I would tell Gini exactly what was going on, but not right now because I needed her to be completely focused.

"Listen babe, I want you to make sure that you're careful with that phone because we can't afford for you to go to the hole," I said.

"I know that Leroy, I'm not dumb."

"I never said that you were. Does your celly know that you have it?" I asked.

"No, and when the time comes, I'll give it to Melonie if we can't take her with us."

"What?" Charlene and I asked in unison.

I could tell that Charlene was just as surprised as I was because her sexual teasing was quickly forgotten, and she was moving towards me.

"L, you know that Melonie is like family…and you don't abandon family."

"Virginia, do you understand that this man is about to risk his life and everything in it for you?" Charlene asked, snatching the phone from my hand.

"Yes Charlene, I get that and-."

"If you get it, then stop trying to save anybody other than your damn self because I'm telling you now that any woman would kill, and die, to have your dude, so don't take what you have for granted," she said, disconnecting the call.

Before I could respond to her unexpected tirade, she walked over to the sink, dropped the phone down the drain and turned on the garbage disposal. The metal blades at the bottom of the sink chewed the hard plastic up in seconds, leaving me stunned by how quickly shit had gone left. I sat speechless as she swiftly made me a plate of food, and brought it to me. She sat it on the counter in front of me and turned to leave, but the tears that I saw in her eyes made me reach out and grab her arm. There was no resistance when I pulled her towards me and wrapped her in my embrace,

"What's going on Charlene?"

"I just hate when a great man is not properly appreciated because they are SO hard to find," she replied.

"I understand, but you don't gotta worry about that because Gini appreciates me. She just has a big heart."

"Honestly L, I don't give a fuck because I appreciate you," she stated boldly, looking me square in the eye.

"I know you do sweetheart."

When I leaned in to kiss her, I was met with a hunger that was about more than food, but I didn't mind. We shared a moment of electricity that had us swaying to music no one could hear, and the only thing that stopped the escalation was my phone going off. I could tell by the way that Charlene hold on to me that she was under the same assumption that I was about who was on the other end of my open line. I knew that avoidance would only cause an issue though, which is why I pulled the phone from my pocket and answered the call without looking.

"Yeah?"

"L-Boogie, what's going on ruler?" IG asked.

Hearing his voice made me extract myself from Charlene's grip, but I didn't push her away.

"What's good bruh?" I replied.

"I'm just letting you know we're in town and you've got the 7-city rulers and rich city rulers at your full disposal. Once the mission is complete, the Louisville Rulers will meet you at the Kentucky line and ride with you across the state. Every state you cross into has a chapter of Rulers, so you will be assisted every step of the way until you're out of the country. From there, we'll rely on the support of our allies, and I don't even have to tell you how fast our network is. You and your will be good bruh, that's my word," he vowed.

"Thank you bruh, I mean that."

"Thought is ruler," he said.

"And Ruler is supreme," I replied, disconnecting the call.

"Is everything okay?" Charlene asked.

"Yeah. My men are in town for what we're about to do."

"How will I know when it's going down?" she asked.

"You won't know until shit kicks off, but don't worry because you'll be secured inside of the medical building. Just go about your job and save as many lives as you can."

"I will, I told you from the beginning that I'd play my position and that position is whatever you need me to be," she said.

"I know you will babe, which is why we need to discuss the next phase of my plan."

"What do you need me to do Leroy?"

I put my phone in my pocket so that I could cup her face in my palms, and stare deep into her eyes in search of the absolute loyalty that I needed could be seen. I kissed her softly, yet thoroughly while enjoying the light remnants of the wine on her tongue. When I could feel the heat of her body radiating hard enough to seep through my clothing, I pulled back to gaze longingly at her.

"I need the ultimate sacrifice from you Charlene."

"Anything," she whispered huskily.

"I need you to take the life of a bad man."

For a moment, her eyes lost focus and she was staring through me, but she quickly snapped back.

"I'll take the life of whatever bad man you need Leroy…if you give life to a good woman."

Chapter 12
2022

"Can I wash your back?" I asked, staring intently into her eyes.

The mixed emotions that she was battling were obvious to see, but I could see past that to the growing love that she felt. There were only a few seconds of hesitation before she passed me the body sponge and shower gel. I took both, then waited while she turned around and moved her hair to the side. I stepped up to her and kissed her at the top of her spine. The shiver that raced through her body gave a visual reaction to the goosebumps that suddenly popped up on her soft skin.

I wanted to create those sensations all over her body but first, I intended to build the suspense some more. After creating a nice lather with the sponge and sweet-smelling body gel, I put the bottle down, and slowly ran the sponge across her upper back and shoulders. Her breathing remained steady even as I worked my way down her spine to the dip right above her ass cheeks. It was my pleasure to take my time washing one ass cheek and then another, but she made sure to tempt my restraint by putting her hands on the wall in front of her and tooting her ass up.

I responded in kind by gently washing her inner thighs before moving up to her pussy. I made sure to rub her clit before dragging the sponge through her pussy lips and up in between her ass cheeks until I was back at the sexy dip right above her cheeks. When I pulled her back against my chest, I could hear the labor in her breathing, and it made me smile. Wrapping my arms around her made it possible for me to run the sponge up and down the front of her body and I made sure to do it slower than a Heinz ketchup commercial. When I tweaked her nipple, she exhaled a moan while grinding her ass against my rock-hard dick, forcing me to swallow spit in my mouth as I fought for composure.

To my way of thinking, this was the opening move to our chess game, but then, she changed the game when she reached behind her and grabbed my dick. She laid her head against my chest and stared up into my eyes in an obvious challenge with her mouth open. I kissed her possessively and she gave me the same energy right back. Her mouth alone was so intoxicating that I was quickly on the brink of giving in, but she suddenly stopped and pulled away from me. The first warning was this mischief that suddenly flooded her eyes to match the smile spreading across her face.

"You want this pussy L?"

"Don't play Luna."

"Answer the question," she insisted. Swatting my hand away when I reached for her.

We both knew how this would end, so the real question was, would I play the game."Can you repeat the question?"

"Do you-want this-pussy-Leroy?"

The fact that one of her hands was caressing one of her titties and nipple while the other was rubbing her clit had my mouth dry as a muthafucka and my dick aching to spear her.

"I-I want it," I replied, already moving closer to her.

Her hand shot out and made firm contact with my chest stopping me in place.

"If you want the pleasures of my pussy, mouth and ass, then you have to work for it," she said moving her hand to my shoulder and applying pressure.

I smiled and nodded my head while kneeling in front of her. She swiftly threw her right leg up on my left shoulder giving me a spectacular view of her neatly trimmed pussy.

The sponge in my hand was dropped and forgotten as I filled both of my palms with her ass cheeks and pulled her closer. Even though I'd only sampled the flavor of her deliciousness by way of her sucking her own cum off my dick and kissing me, I could identify her nectar with my eyes closed.

My lips locked on her clit like a bank vault slamming shut and before she knew what hither, I was ringing her alarm. I licked and sucked on her pussy until the leg she was standing on was shaking harder than a stripper whose rent was due. her moans were flowing from her mouth like synchronized swimmers, but I pushed them to the level of Olympic gold when I slipped a hand in between her ass cheeks. I only put the tip of my finger in her asshole, but that was enough to make her cream in my mouth like a melting ice cream cone.

I made sure to suck her climax out of her and begin the rebuild before I stopped and got up off my knees. When we were standing eye to eye, I could see her mounting hunger and that signaled the end of playing for her. I pulled her to me roughly, picked her up and thrust my dick inside of her still quivering pussy walls.

"Fuck. Fuck me like you mean it," she demanded.

I started to slam her against one of the walls surrounding us, but instead, I left the water running and carried her back into the bedroom.

"Wait-wait L, let's stay in the shower."

"I got this bae, just hold on," I replied, laying her on the mattress.

My first stroke stopped at the base of her stomach and had her eyes rolling back while her lashes fluttered like the curtains on an open window. The follow-up had the same effect and before she knew it, I'd set a rhythm more lethal than a boxing speed bag.

"L-L-L," she chanted while raking her nails across my back.

The feeling of her pussy sucking me in over and over felt like a vortex had married a black hole, and I was stuck in their quicksand. I was so lost in the moment that I almost missed the warning bells going off in my head, but my instincts took over and I froze.

"L don't stop-."

"Shush," I said clapping my hand firmly over her mouth.

The look in her eyes was still one of playful sexiness in need of the fulfillment that was just around the corner, but it quickly changed when she heard the noise that I had. The only person who has a key to my spot was my sister and she could've doubled back to talk to me, but something inside of me told me that someone different was in my crib.

I waited, not moving, but listening intently to see if my instincts were on point. After a full 60 seconds I still wasn't hearing anything out of the ordinary, so I started moving slowly inside Luna without taking my hand away from her mouth. It only took a few deep dives before the fear vanished from her eyes, and the hunger replaced it. I didn't play any games with her this time, I fucked her hard and fast until her pussy spasmed in sync with my dick, and we came in strangled grunts. My dick hadn't stopped spitting cum inside her when my peripheral vision caught sight of something, and I grabbed Luna as I rolled off the far side of my bed.

The sound of silenced shots muffled the sounds of us hitting the floor, but I was only paying attention to grabbing the Glock that hit the floor with us. The moment that my finger wrapped around the rubber grip a masked face appeared at the foot of my bed and I wasted no time pointing and shooting. He fired at the same time and based on Luna's screams I knew that she was hit. Two shots from me dropped the first nigga but four more eyes and two mouths appeared right behind him and the shit they were shooting was fully automatic.

My finger danced on the trigger faster than Gregory Hines, but I still felt the searing burn in my thigh from a bullet hitting its mark. I fought the urge to get up, instead choosing to wait in case there were more hittas looking to punch my ticket. It felt like I was holding my breath for the full 2 minutes that I lay there, and it wasn't until I wanted to move that I realized Luna wasn't screaming anymore. She wasn't moving either. When I used my right hand to lift her head off my chest, I could feel her blood oozing in between my fingers, so the lifeless look in her eyes didn't surprise me, but I still pushed her body off of me and slowly climbed to my feet with my gun at the ready.

When I didn't see any more immediate threats, I took a moment to examine this wound on my thigh. The bullet had missed my main artery, but the hole was still big enough for me to stick my pinky through that muthafucka, which meant stitches were necessary. That was a secondary problem when compared to how the fuck I was gonna get out of having 4 dead bodies in my house. My first order of business was to make sure everyone was actually dead, and once that was done, I got something to stop me from bleeding all over the place. My next move was to call IG and Zuk because I definitely needed assistance!

The thing I appreciated about real niggas was that they didn't ask senseless questions or waste time with the dumb shit. I said I needed help and IG assured me that the Calvary was coming. I pulled on a pair of shorts and grabbed the matching Glock .17 with the 30-round clip and posted up on the couch like I was waiting for the end of days. Forty-Five minutes later, a knock at the door rattled my already shattered nerves, causing me to jump. There was a dull throb already settling into my thigh, but I pushed through the pain to get up and answer the door.

"What happened?" IG asked immediately.

I stepped to the side so that he and Zuk could enter my apartment and then I pointed to the bedroom in the back. Both men headed in that direction and by the time they returned, I was back in my spot on the couch trying to figure out what my next move was.

"What happened?" IG repeated.

"They came in shooting while I was fucking ole girl and I got lucky enough to kill them before they got me."

"Pack up all traces of you being here right now and give me the gun that you used," Zuk demanded, holding his hand out.

"Can you ride?" IG asked.

"Yeah, but I got my car outside."

"I know that, but you need to vanish without a trace, and someone will remember your car. So, you're gonna put my helmet on and take my bike," IG replied.

For a moment I was dumbstruck just standing there looking at the helmet he was extending to me. Nobody wore IG's predator headgear or rode that particular bike because it was like his personal calling card. One universal truth about IG was that he had hurt a muthafucka-down predator style and that was the end of your existence. Almost all of us had that mentality, which was part of the reason we were chosen, but it still felt weird to be trusted with something so personal. I accepted the helmet and then we all got to work. Within 10 minutes, I had the safe emptied of everything and had my backpack on my back with its contents secured.

"Give me your house keys and leave your phone here in the safe, so your GPS location won't contradict what we tell the people," Zuk said.

"Okay, but what are you gonna say?" I asked.

Zuk and IG exchanged a look before they both looked at me.

"We've already hit up one of our ladies from the women's chapter of Rulers, and someone will be here shortly. The story is that she was house sitting and she brought a girl back from a bar around the corner. They had fun last night and this morning somebody broke in to rob the place which led to their demise. The gun ain't dirty and it's a mandatory requirement that all of our females be licensed and trained to possess a firearm, so that's not a problem. We'll set the stage and then disappear to let it play out how it needs to from there. It's simple," IG replied.

"How do I explain my connection to the woman here in my spot that's house sitting whenever the cops get around to questioning me?" I asked.

"You tell the truth, that she's a member of the club," Zuk replied.

"We got this L, but you need to hop on the predator and get gone because we're already fucking with the window for time of death. Too big of an unexplained discrepancy will throw the story off," IG reasoned.

I nodded my head because I knew he was right but as I took a step towards the front door, I stopped and looked back towards my bedroom.

"They had on masks," I said.

"Huh?" IG asked.

"They had on masks, and I didn't even think to take them off to see who the fuck was trying to kill me because I was too worried about going back to jail again. I gotta know though," I replied heading back to my bedroom.

I checked the bodies I dropped together before moving to the first nigga who'd come through the door. I didn't know the first two in the slightest, but when I saw what remained of the last man, my heart hit my feet. The last time I'd seen him, I couldn't quite place his face in my memory but somehow, seeing him in death unlocked that door inside me.

"Yo, we got a fucking problem," I said feeling a touch of panic.

"Why?" Zuk asked.

"Because that lieutenant Steven Hogan formally of the D.C Police force. He's Mercedes' other baby daddy, and the nigga responsible for me being locked up last time because he alerted VA that I was in D.C," I replied.

"So, you just killed a cop?" IG asked.

"Yeah, I guess I did."

Chapter 13
2027

I slid into the booth at the waffle house across from IG and sat my helmet right next to his trademark predator helmet.

"You eating?" he asked.

"Nah, I'm good, but I need some coffee to wake me up."

"I bet you do nigga, you look like Charlene drained all the cum out your ass," he replied, laughing as he signaled the waitress.

"The woman can take dick bruh, and she ain't ashamed of that particular talent. As long as she does exactly what I need her to do then it's all good, and I'll get her pregnant."

The way his eyebrows shot up told me that I definitely said more than I'd intended to.

"Don't even ask, just tell me we're ready to go," I said quickly.

"Oh, we're definitely ready we're just waiting on you to raise the curtain on this show."

I checked the time on my watch and saw that it was a little after 3 a.m., which meant that the penitentiary was still slumbering like most people in the world. I knew from experience that most Correctional Officers were fighting with all their might to stay awake right now, and that meant their senses were as dull as a butter knife. It was time to wake that ass up.

"Make the call," I stated, pulling out my own phone to contact my DMV Rulers.

I knew that my chapter of the Ruler nation was ready, so once I shot the text message, I sat back comfortably. A cute waitress appeared and filled my coffee cup up before placing two menus on the table and retreating.

I dint give the menu a second glance, but I grabbed the coffee and ingested it as quickly as the heat of it would allow. Before I got halfway through my first cup, my phone was going off demanding my attention. My text messages revealed that Charlene had arrived at work to make sure Gini was in medical, and Sarah was on her post in Gini's pod. That meant the pieces were in play and all that was left was to take action.

"Let's go," I said standing up and digging a few bills out of my pocket to pay for the coffee.

IG followed my lead, and we grabbed our helmets while heading for the door.

"Stay close because we're moving fast, and when you see me change from using my regular headlight to my night vision one, you do the same," I instructed.

"I got you," he replied, hopping on his bike.

Our mode of transportation offered us a certain amount of stealth capabilities and the fact that every Ruler in the nation had a navigation system embedded in their bike with night vision, only increased that. It gave us a slight advantage against the OPS, no matter who we were moving against. I hopped on my bike and led the way off into the night.

The route we were taking was one that I'd run so many times that I could drive it blindfolded, so I had my bike singing at 90mph quickly. I could feel the predator's presence right behind me because that bike was a fine-tuned animal that hugged the pavement like roadkill. It only took 12 minutes to make it to the prison, and as soon as I came to a stop alongside the road, I spotted other shadows that were similar to mine. It was obvious that the Rulers owned the night. I pressed a button on the bottom of my helmet to turn on my microphone and address the nation.

"Testing, Testing. All Rulers check in and count off," I stated.

IG led off with the roll call, and I finished it up a couple of minutes later with a grand total of 214 Rulers on deck for the block party.

"Demolition team, you're up," I said.

"One minute out," came the reply.

Less than 60 seconds later, I felt the ground trembling before I heard the rumbling angry diesel engines.

"Lewy, cut the power and jam the signals. We're going in," I said.

"Copy that L."

A few seconds later, the lights of the entire Fluvanna Correctional Center flickered, and then went out like the Titanic sinking. The hulking structure f steel and razor wire looked more menacing in the moonlight, but it was beautiful, nonetheless. I pulled out my twin black Beretta 9mm's that I'd had converted to fully automatic and made sure both 40-round clips were secured.

The headlights from the two 18-wheelers heading in my direction illuminated the road on both sides allowing me to see nothing but Rulers with weapons everywhere. The trucks stopped side by side about 100ft past mine and IG's location, which effectively blocked off three roads at the four-lane intersection. Once the trucks were in position, the stolen military tanks that had been driving behind them came to a stop and angled their guns at both guard towers on this side of the prison.

"In position L," Demon said.

"Open the door and let them out," I replied.

Moments later the night was awash with fire and the ground rattled like an earthquake had awoken it as the guard towers collapsed into a pile of rubble. Before all the debris hit the ground the tanks were moving forward, knocking down the fence and taking aim at the remaining towers across the compound.

"Shoot anything in uniform," I said, jogging towards the black hole backlit by the moon.

The first thing that I saw was a Correctional Officer struggling to his feet, but a quick tap of the trigger from me put him back on his face.

"I'm right behind you l," IG said.

Once we actually crossed onto the prison grounds, I took off at a dead sprint, shooting anyone that wasn't a Ruler or allies along the way. I'd studied the layout of Fluvanna until I could see it in my sleep, so I led the way to the medical building and made it there inside in 30 seconds. No time was wasted when it came to trying to persuade the Correctional Officers to let us in because I immediately lobbed a grenade at the door and took cover.

The blast brought heat and screams of agony but neither fazed me as I led the way with the fire and twisted metal. The lifeless eyes of the night shift Correctional Officers looked up at me from right inside what was left of the door, but I stepped over their bodies and headed for the back.

"I got eyes on the front, go get her," IG said.

"Evac in 2 minutes," I replied moving faster towards the door at the end of the hallway I was on.

When I got to my location, I tapped on the door twice, and Charlene pulled it open swiftly. We exchanged a look of pure understanding and then she side-stepped so that I was standing face to face with my reason for breathing. I barely got a good look at Gini before she took a Lambeau Leap into my arms and hugged me fiercely.

"I wanna kiss you so bad right now and give you some of this good pussy right here," she said.

I chuckled at that, a while caressing her big booty with my pistol.

"We can take care of that in a little while, but if it's ok with you I'd like to complete the mission of getting you out of here," I replied.

The pout on her face was sexy, but she didn't argue. She dropped a quick kiss on my helmet's visor, dropped to her feet and took one of the guns from my hand.

"I'm ready when you are my husband."

"Charlene, go to the cafeteria and keep your head down," I instructed, pulling Gini into the hallway behind me.

I retraced my steps moving with even more purpose because I could see freedom in the night sky ahead.

"Lewy, we're coming out, send in the drone," I said.

"Copy that L, coming in hot."

By the time I, Gini and IG made it to the sidewalk outside of medical, it looked like the sun had risen because there were flames dancing everywhere. Buildings were falling in spectacular fashion, rivaling scenes from movie sets, but the screams of dying women were real enough to give me chills. I really hadn't wanted to kill any female inmate but in order for my plan to succeed, there had to be sacrifices made. I gave Gini's hand a reassuring squeeze when I saw the despair flood her eyes at the sight of some of the buildings falling. I understand her pain at this moment, but I knew that I could replace that sooner than later with joy and love she had never known.

"Come on," I said, interlocking her fingers with my own and taking off at a dead run.

The sounds of gunfire reached my ears right before two shadows moved on my right side, but by the time my mind registered the threat, Gini had reacted by letting off enough shots to turn both figures into lawn fertilizer. More shots could be heard in the distance, but my focus was on the gate in front of us.

"Ruler's let's move!" I demanded.

It took less than a minute to reach my bike and I stood guard while Gini put my extra helmet on.

"Infraredscan Lewy, make sure we're all out and then level the medical building," I said.

"Copy that L."

I hopped on my bike and passed Gini my pistol before telling her to get on behind me. By that time, IG had his helmet on and his bike was idling next to mine. When I nodded that I was ready he signaled that he was taking over the airwaves now.

"Rulers, split up and fan out. Those of you that were already selected for the second half of this mission know what to do, so let's go. Lewy, are we good yet?" IG asked.

"All clear Prez, but I've got state police helicopter coming inbound from the southwest."

"Knock it out the sky," IG replied, without hesitation.

Ten seconds later the sky in front of us lit up in a ball of orange that resembled an angry pumpkin.

"Load the trucks," IG demanded.

Bikes started moving past us, while other Rulers headed in different directions that created a scene of organized chaos. IG spun his bike around, and I followed his lead so that we could bring up the rear of the bikes going up the ramp of one of the 18-wheelers. When I brought my bike to a stop, the door shut behind me and a few minutes later, we pulled off slowly.

I knew the truck would split up once we got closer to the highway, and we'd already determined which truck would follow which route. After 15 minutes of movement, I got off my bike and collected my pistols from a still-trembling Gini.

"Did-Did you *really* just break me out of prison?" she asked, in awe.

The lighting in the back of the big rig was dim at best, but I could still see the tears welling up in my wife's eyes.

"I told you that I was coming for you baby. Did you ever doubt me?" I asked, tucking my guns and pulling her into my arms.

"To be honest Leroy, I did have a little doubt because it would take a nigga who's certifiable to pull off the shit that you did."

"Or just a nigga who loves you that much," I countered, sincerely.

When I said that, her tears surged past the Levey; she'd been holding them behind and spilled down her cheeks like midnight rain. I brought my lips to hers gently and kissed her in understanding entwined with love. All my life, I'd wanted someone to bet on me like I had on her, so I understood the doubt and I could only imagine the fear that she'd felt waking up every morning knowing that death was her only escape from prison. How she'd been able to maintain the 17 years that she had on the inside; I'd never know.

All I know from this point forward was that if she died, it would be beside me in the streets and not behind a chain-link fence. I could feel the temperature rising in our kiss, which made me pull back because I wasn't about to dick my wife down in front of my squad.

"You pussy," she said, laughing and playfully punching me in the chest.

"We'll see about that later slim, just keep the same energy," I replied.

"Oh, I got plenty of energy baby, you just make sure that you can keep up. So, what happens next?"

I found it hard to answer her question simply because she had her hand inside my pants, and she was squeezing my dick like it was a chew toy. I cleared my throat to focus, but I maintained steady eye contact with her grinning ass.

"We're headed for the state line, as we should cross over into Kentucky in a few hours. We'll be met by more of my people, and they'll lead us across the state until we're free of that commonwealth as well," I replied.

"Won't it be more dangerous to roll through a commonwealth with my face plastered on every news station from here to Singapore?"

"Babe, nobody searches for dead people," I said confidently.

"What are you talking about Leroy, I'm clearly not dead," she stated, squeezing my dick more firmly.

"You're right, but you're not seeing the big picture sweetheart. By the time the sun rises, they would think you're dead and gone, and the best part is that Pony will be blamed for it."

Chapter 14
2022

The silence in the room was deafening and then IG gave me the slow smile accompanied by the trademark gravel-infused voice of his.

"This ain't the first cop to die at the hands of a Ruler," IG said.

"And it won't be the last," Zuk stated calmly.

"We'll take care of it, you just go establish your alibi," IG instructed.

It didn't feel right to leave my men here holding the bag while I skated, but I knew that I had to go. I left my apartment and took the stairs to avoid too much camera traffic. I made sure that I had the predator helmet on the entire time even though I knew that the security footage would be sanitized before the cops got a hold of it. Ideally, I would've simply had the camera data erased, but I needed the arrival of the hittas to be documented in case my freedom was threatened over this shit.

Once I got to IG's bike, I sent my nigga Lewy a text briefing him on the situation and giving him instructions before I hopped on and jetted off into the afternoon sun. At first, I had no destination in mind; just the desire to put space in between myself and what happened, but then, the image of my sister's unexpected visit popped into my head. I needed to address the issue of my children and be an actual father instead of just a street nigga. With that in mind, I pointed the bike in the direction of Lia's apartment, and I opened the throttle wide.

I pulled up outside her building 30 minutes later and went straight to her ground floor apartment with the predator helmet still on.

"What the fuck?" Lia said, opening the door before I could knock properly.

Once I pulled my helmet off, she relaxed the gripped on the .380 Ruger clutched in her right hand.

"I'd heard you were out," she said, walking away from the door and back into the apartment.

I took that as my invitation to come in, but the chilliness of her welcome home reception was impossible to misinterpret. I closed the door behind me and followed the sound of the TV coming from down the hallway. When I stepped into the living room, I was hit with the surprise of finding my other daughter sitting beneath a thick cloud of smoke on the couch beside Lia.

Cyn's eyes met mine, and they flickered to the .380 Lia had sat on the coffee table in front of them. The instant sweat that I felt in my palms was alarming because my body and subconscious weren't contemplating shooting my own child. When her eye's met mine, I could see the thought of picking up the gun travel across her forehead like the jumbotron at a football game. She wisely didn't reach for the weapon, which allowed me to fight the temptation to put my own pistol in my hand for comfort.

"Cyn I'm sorry," I stated genuinely.

"You're really not, but whatever," she replied.

"Sis," Lia said, tapping her on her leg while shaking her head.

I felt grateful to have Lia trying to keep shit calm, but I knew that the fire sign of Aries in my younger daughter would win out eventually. The trick for me was to be gone before it did.

"I'm sorry I didn't tell you two myself that I was out, but I wanted to come home quietly this time," I explained, looking directly at Lia.

"Yeah, well a limo and a white bitch ain't exactly inconspicuous my nigga," Cyn said sarcastically.

My eyes immediately swung to her, but the question of how she knew what she knew stopped on my tongue. Barely.

"You paying attention to the wrong shit, and that's probably why your life is in a bit of disarray right now," I replied.

"That's uncalled for pops," Lia said quickly.

Cyn's eyes went to the pistol in front of her again, and the smile that spread across her face was sinister, yet beautiful. It was her mother's smile. I was just about to tell her that when I saw the slight shifting of her eyes, which coincided with the hair on the back of my neck standing up, I didn't have to turn around to know that someone was behind me, and I knew without a doubt just who it was.

"What's poppin Rome?" I asked, still staring intently at Cyn.

"Do I know you nigga?" he replied aggressively.

"If you don't fix your tone I'ma be your first pallbearer," I stated calmly.

I kept my eyes on Cyn, so I noticed the barely perceptible shake of the head that she gave Rome to discourage whatever foolish shit his young mind was concocting. I wasn't worried in the slightest though, especially because I'd seen Lia clutching a second pistol in my peripheral vision, and I knew it wasn't intended for me. A few seconds passed before Rome stepped from behind me and made his grand entrance. I quickly sized up the 6'0, 180lbs. brown skin nigga with the babyface, searching to see if he had the balls to be King of the jungle, he was playing in. His brown eyes didn't give me a definite yes, but I saw the potential.

"You're her father," Rome said, nodding in understanding now.

"No, I'm both their fathers," I corrected.

"My bad. I didn't think I'd get to meet you though because somebody told me that you were dead."

"Wishful thinking, I guess," I replied, smiling to hide my curiosity over his statement.

My third eye was tracking his energy to discern whether or not he's been threatening me in the way passive/aggressive niggas did and when I glanced at Lia, I could tell that she was doing the same.

"Who said our dad was dead?" Lia asked.

"The streets talk," Cyn replied before Rome could.

"Oh yeah? How do you know that when you don't speak that language?" Lia countered.

Cyn shot a look at her sister that almost made me laugh, but I didn't wanna be an antagonist. Rome didn't have that problem though, so his snickering came out loud and clear much to Cyn's embarrassment. The flush that highlighted her cheeks was more obvious than a glowing Santa Claus on somebody's front porch, and it made me feel bad for my baby.

"From what I hear, you ain't fluent in that language either, Lil nigga, so I don't know why you're laughing. Cyn's a reflection of you," I reminded him.

His laughter dried up quicker than a fiend's understanding during a crack drought, but the smile on my face came from the look of relief filling Cyn's eyes.

The wrong words were on the tip of young Rome's tongue, but he did the right thing by keeping his lips closed.

"Let's go babe," Cyn said, standing up and moving around the table towards him.

When she took his hand there was only a moment's hesitation before he allowed himself to be led from the room.

114

With Lia and I left alone, she visibly relaxed, and let the other gun go.

"You really know how to make an entrance Pops."

"Sorry. I'm in a bad mood, but getting shot will do that to a nigga," I replied, moving over to the seat Cyn had vacated so that I could sit down.

Taking some of the pressure off my leg eased the ache I was feeling, but it didn't take it completely away.

"Did you get shot, or did you get shot at?"

"I know the difference Lia, and I said what I said."

"Are you ok? Where did you get hit?" she asked, full of concern.

"My leg, and I think I need a few stitches."

"You can explain what happened while I sew you up. Come on," she said, standing up.

I followed her to one of the two bathrooms in the apartment and sat on the toilet while she gathered the necessary supplies.

"Strip and start talking," she demanded, kneeling in front of me.

I complied and ran down what my morning had been like. She worked quickly and efficiently sewing up my wound in less than 10 minutes.

"Where did you learn to do that?" I asked, impressed by the results and the steadiness of her hands.

"Nursing is what I'm in school for, Pops, or did you forget?"

"Nah, I just thought you were learning how to take care of old people or something," I replied sheepishly.

"And why would that be the only thing I learn?"

"Because you better not ever think about putting my ass in an old folk's home when I can't wipe my own ass!" I stated, laughing.

She laughed with me, but I could see the concern in her eyes still.

"Are you sure you're gonna make it to that age Pop?"

My natural response was one of Bravado and Arrogance, but I knew it would be disrespectful to insult her intelligence after what had just happened.

"I've made a lot of enemies sweetheart, so there's a chance that one of them could get lucky enough to punch my ticket one day. Today ain't that day though, and I'm not gonna stop living over the possibility that I might die because I'm guaranteed to meet death eventually. It's all about how you meet him though. When it's y time to meet death, I fully intend to do it with a smile on my face, and the knowledge in my mind that I'm leaving a legacy worthy of the time spent here. Feel me?"

"I feel you Pops, but I still want you to be more careful. You killed a cop, and if that ever comes to light, your life will be over either way you cut it. I don't wanna lose you," she said softly.

I pulled her into my arms and hugged her in a way that I wished I'd had the opportunity to do for her entire life. Due to the circumstances that we couldn't have controlled, we'd lost a lifetime of memories, and neither of us was content with only having the time we'd spent together thus far, counting for all that we'd ever get. So, I'd move more carefully, and at the same time, I'd spend more time with my kids.

"How long has your sister been here?" I asked, pulling back and looking down at Lia.

"Ever since her mom died. I did my best to help her through that part of her life, but she's got that nigga in her ear feeding her bullshit."

"Yeah, your aunt Byrd pulled up on me this morning and said something about that. She seems to think that eliminating ole boy will free you, and change her life for the better," I replied.

"I agree, but the nigga is gang-affiliated Pops and them blood niggas ain't playing with nobody out in these streets."

"My niggas ain't playing neither, but we understand that money is more powerful than any gun made. A lot of people say that money is the root of all evil, instead of just acknowledging the truth, which is that money is the root of life. When you really think about life as a whole and factor in everything including success, growth, stress, and even faith, you can find a common thread. Money. Do you know why? Because money affects change quicker than anything else in this world except God himself. So, that's why money is simply the root, whether that be good or evil," I concluded

Lia stood up and just stared at me for a second before responding.

"You're weird Pops."

We both laughed and then started cleaning up the mess that came from her fixing me up. By the time we made it back to the living room, Cyn was back on the couch, smoking something that smelled enticing enough to have my right eye twitching. There was no sign of the lil nigga, but I knew instinctively that he wasn't too far away.

"I got a bottle of Cîroc Brandy Pop, and I'ma pour you a shot to take the edge off," Lia said.

I was gonna ask her what she was doing with liquor under the legal age, but I recognized the moment alone she was trying to give me with Cyn, so I focused on that and just nodded in agreement. When Lia left the room, I took a seat beside Cyn on the couch and contemplated my next move.

"Don't bother saying that you're sorry my mom is dead because we both know that bullshit."

"Why do you assume that, Cyn?" I asked, looking over at her.

"Because you didn't fuck with my mom. You viewed her as your OPP for leaving you while you were locked up, which shows how fucked up you truly are because you couldn't even let her live her life. You moved on, so you should've let her do the same."

"I didn't give two fucks about your mom moving on Cyn. What her and I had was old news, so I don't know where you're getting your info, but it's inaccurate," I replied.

"Of course, you're gonna say that! Everybody knows that you're still fucked up over my mom, which was why your petty ass wouldn't forgive her when she begged you for that shit! It's your fault she's dead, and now her kids have to grow up without a mother."

"Cyn, you didn't know-."

My lips suddenly freeze in their motion of passing along my explanation as my mind suddenly jumped ship to an entirely different mode of thought. My daughter's thoughts sounded eerily familiar and when I connected that with the knowledge she had about why her mom committed suicide, I had a theory to work with.

"Here you go Pop," Lia said, coming back into the room and passing me a peanut butter jar half full of dark liquor.

I accepted it and took a healthy swig before attempting to pass it back to Lia.

"Nah, old man that's you," she said snickering.

I took another sip and sat it on the table so that I could take my backpack off. I unzipped it and pulled out my favorite gun to conceal on me along with my box of hollow-point bullets so that I could reload the pistol with these bullets only.

"What's that Pops?" Lia asked.

"It's a 9mm Hellcat OSP," I replied.

"Damn, that little ass piece is a 9mm? how many bullets does it hold, 4?" Lia asked, laughing.

"Try 14 smartass, 14 in the clip and one in the head," I replied, ejecting bullets as we spoke.

She watched with open fascination as I switched out the standard bullets for the hollows and when it was done, I slid it into my pants pocket.

"Do you think it's a good idea to ride around with a bag full of guns and shit?" Lia asked, looking down into my backpack.

"Nah it ain't smart, it's simply necessary at the moment until I regroup. Don't worry lil one, I always bounce back, and it's gonna take more than some crooked police to shake me," I replied.

"Crooked police?" Cyn asked.

She'd tried to ask the question on some real nonchalant shit, but she didn't realize I'd baited her, so I was watching her closely, she was nervous.

"Yeah, some crooked cops tried to kill me this morning at my spot and one of them even managed to shoot me," I said.

"Damn, that's crazy...I see you managed to escape, though. The cops probably got away too, huh?" she asked, probing gently.

Before I could answer her question, I heard the sounds of Kevin Gates rapping about fucking with the plugs daughter and I realized this was her ringtone. When she pulled her phone out, I had expected her to answer it, but instead, she stared at the screen for what seemed like an eternity.

"Everything okay Cyn? You look like you just got some bad news," I said, smirking.

When she looked up at me, her eyes were clouded by devastation and loss with a hint of panic trying to peek through.

"D-Daddy I-."

"Shhh, Cyn," I said, holding up my hand.

I could tell that she wanted to finish whatever she'd intended to say, but Rome suddenly burst into the room.

"Bae, Steve is dead."

Chapter 15
2027
(3 hours later)

"….In breaking news overnight, we've learned that Fluvanna Correctional Center in Virginia was attacked. Be warned that the pictures we're about to show you are graphic in content….as you could see, it looks like satellite images from a middle Eastern war zone instead of the secure women's prison it was some hours ago. I'm told that the authorities are unsure at this time as to whether this was a daring prison break fit for a James Bond movie, or a simple yet calculated attack on our female prison system. Governor Dowell-Wilson has the same questions naturally, but right now, the priority is making sure the remaining prisoners are safe and secure in case another attack is imminent.

When this Channel 6 reporter had the chance to ask the Governor a question, I asked whether or not all the prisoners were accounted for. The Governor side-stepped that line of inquiry and focused on how heinous this act was. I think everyone can agree that the act is indeed deplorable because no matter what these women have done, they're still human beings, and they didn't deserve to be slaughtered like animals. The monsters responsible for this are out there somewhere and the help of the general public is needed.

If you have any information about the attack on Fluvanna Correctional Center, you're encouraged to call the number at the bottom of the screen. Reporting live, this is Lydia Foster, Channel 6 News…."

When the screen on my phone went black, Gini passed my phone back and leaned her head against my shoulder. We'd both been paying close attention to all the news feeds ever since we'd climbed off my bike inside the truck and sat down together in a corner of the fast-moving tractor-trailer. The sounds of others whispering around us reminded us that we weren't alone, but other than that, we were in a cocoon of our making.

There was so much I wanted to say to my wife, but I was forced to communicate in silence because I could tell that this was a bitter-sweet moment for her. I understood all too well the bonds that were formed when you were forced to share time and space in a cage with others and so I could feel the pain that he felt over losing some of her friends. No names had been released yet, but she'd seen the buildings that I'd reduced to rubble, so she knew who'd died.

The last thing I'd wanted was to hurt her, but if I had to do it all over again, I'd do it the same way. Having her beside me close enough to feel her body heat meant more to me than any life I had taken or would take and even though I knew she understood that it was love pushing me, I still couldn't say all of this to her. All I could do was love her silently, but I was content to do that because at least, she was free.

"We're 10 minutes out L," IG called from the shadows.

"Got it," I replied.

"10 minutes from where?" Gini asked.

"From the rendezvous point where we'll meet up with some friends, and head into Kentucky," I replied.

"Why Kentucky? Where are you taking me, husband?"

"I'm taking you to safety sweetheart, so all you gotta do is trust me," I said, standing up and pulling her to her feet.

"You know that I trust you with my life Leroy, I was just curious about what you had planned for us."

I leaned down and kissed her gently, making sure to nibble on her bottom lip because I knew that would make her pussy wet enough to drown several fish.

"Why are you trying to start some shit?" she asked huskily.

I laughed softly while sliding my hand down inside the front of her tight-fitting sweatpants and gently massaging her clit through the softness of her cotton panties. The feeling of her heat radiating from her pussy had my top lip twitching and my dick throbbing in rhythm with the gears of the truck shifting beneath our feet. This was definitely about to spin out of control faster than a Nascar restart.

"Fuck me right here," she demanded, reaching down inside my pants and grabbing my dick.

As badly as I wanted to give her what we both desperately wanted, I knew there was no way to fully enjoy the magic we were sure to create.

"Be patient babe," I replied, pulling my hand out of her pants.

I stepped away from her so that she'd have to let my dick go and I grabbed both helmets off my bike so that we could prepare to ride.

"I've got an idea," she said, smiling mischievously.

"Do I even want to know what's going on in that beautiful, crazy mind of yours babe?"

"Of course, you do because it's crossed your mind before, but you said a muthafucka had to be insane to try it," she replied smiling with even more of a devilish glint in her eyes.

I thought about it for a second and then the lightbulb went off in my head bringing a smile to my face identical to hers. I now knew exactly what she had on her mind, so the only question that remained was would I be bold enough to match her crazy. A quick look around revealed that everyone was getting ready to ride and no one was paying attention to Gini and me. To me, this represented the opportunity of s lifetime and I intended to seize it.

"Hold this," I instructed passing her my helmet before I left her standing next to my bike and went over to IG.

I whispered something to him, causing him to dig something out of his pocket and hand it to me. I returned to Gini and once again checked our immediate surroundings.

"Stand perfectly still, I mean it," I demanded, grabbing ahold of her pants and pulling her towards me.

I reached down in between her thick thighs and took ahold of her pants at the crotch. I cut a slit in her pants with a quick flick of my wrist, and then I went further still by cutting a slit in her panties. All of this was done with my eyes locked on hers and me seeing what I was doing in my mind's eyes. The unwavering trust only made her blue eyes sexier as she stared unflinchingly at me, and I had to remind myself to breathe every few seconds.

Just the mere thought of what I was preparing to try had my dick harder than concrete reinforced by steel, dipped in diamonds. Once I was sure that the holes, I cut would work, I put the knife in my pocket and climbed on my bike. Despite the lust and excitement in her eyes, I could still see the skepticism over whether or not this was physically possible to pull off. If Gini had been any taller or any thicker, it would've been suicidal to try what we were about to pull off, but by my estimation, she was perfect in every way.

"Get on," I demanded.

"You're serious L?"

"You said that your pussy was to die for, so let me find out," I said, smiling as I slid my back a little.

She passed me my helmet before propping hers on top of her head and stepping to the side of my bike so that she could size it up. I unzipped my pants and pulled my shirt down so that no one could see that I'd pulled my dick out. Once Gini saw that, she threw her caution to the wind and climbed up on the bike with her back to the gas tank so that she was wedged between the tank and me.

"Lean back because you're gonna be doing the work for real, but you need to listen to exactly what I'm telling you. Okay?" I asked.

"Yes, my King."

"Good, now wrap your legs around me loosely until I'm inside you," I said, propping my own helmet on top of my head and grabbing my dick.

Even in the shadows, I could see the color in her cheeks signifying her blushing and it was cute. I could feel her body trembling already and I knew that it was a combination of arousal, anticipation and nervousness swimming through her bloodstream. Pushing my dick against her pussy lips had my mouth watering because of how wet she was, but even with her pussy soaking the head of my dick, it was still a fight to penetrate her. I had to work an inch at a time inside of her until I got halfway home and then we ran out of time.

"We're here L. You ready?" IG asked.

"Yeah," I growled through clenched teeth while pushing the rest of me inside Gini hard and fast.

Her sudden gasp was drowned out by the sound of the truck's J-brake engaging but the look of shock and hunger in her eyes was unmistakable.

"Wrap your legs around me tight, and use your leverage to lift your hips. You're in control baby," I whispered, kissing her quickly and pushing her helmet down.

She rotated her hips while squeezing me with her legs and my dick touched her spine to begin our game of tag. I pulled my helmet down and started the bike's engine and said a silent prayer thanking, 'God for the woman I was joined to.' I started talking dirty to Gini, but then, I remembered that our mics were linked to everyone else's.

"Gini, the mic in the helmet is open so the rest of the Rulers can hear our conversation. I just wanted you to be aware," I said.

"F-Fucking asshole," she mumbled, still moving her hips slightly.

I couldn't help the smile on my face, nor the sensations shooting through my body. All I could do was hope I didn't cum and cause us to run into oncoming traffic. A few moments passed with us silently fucking at a steady rhythm without anyone knowing, and I even managed to plant my feet so that I could feed her some strokes that made her back arch.

I could feel the sweat trickling down my nose as I fought my climax, and I knew I had to slow down because sweat in my eyes would definitely fuck us up when we were on the move. Despite my undivided attention being on my wife and what we were doing, I still spotted IG moving in between bikes, headed in our direction.

"Hold still," I whispered.

It was so hard to keep our bodies from attacking each other that I could literally feel her shaking along with me, but we held it together.

"Are you really gonna ride with her like that?" IG asked.

"Yeah, she said that she wants to try it. I'm a pro, so you already know that I got this," I replied confidently.

"Whatever you say my nigga. All I know is that I'ma be pissed off if we went through all that just for you two crazy muthafuckas to end up roadkill. When the door goes up, make sure you stay right behind me, but I'm only riding with you all till you reach the Kentucky line. From there you'll follow our brothers and sisters as you all head Northeast.

Check-in time is 5 pm Eastern standard time every day, and if you miss 2 check-in appointments, we're coming. Take this," he said, handing me something that looked like a 50-cent piece.

"It's a GPS tracker and me and Zuk are the only ones who can access it," gw he explained.

I reached behind me and put it under my seat, guessing correctly that it was magnetic. Based on how the truck had been steadily reducing speed I knew that we'd exited the highway some miles back, but I could still hear the sounds of cars moving fast as we came to a complete stop now. That meant we were at a rest stop off the interstate, and now it was time to cover a lot of ground quickly.

"You sure you can ride like that?" IG asked skeptically.

"I got it bruh," I replied.

He nodded and then went back to his bike.

"Thank God," Gini said, immediately squeezing her legs and pussy muscles at the same time.

It was hard to breathe for a few seconds, but then I used the motion of me putting my kickstand up to dive deep onto her pussy and really pin her ass up against the gas tank.

"L," she exclaimed.

I chuckled while reeving the engine to give her some noise for her to harmonize with. The sudden sounds of bikes coming to life all around us caused a much-needed distraction, and all it took was a few good strokes before she was releasing a torrent of pussy juices all over my dick.

I could hear her teeth chattering in my ear as she fought verbal confirmation that her world was breaking apart at the seams, and it excited me. By the time the back door was lifted, I was leaning down on top of her so that she could hold on tight, while we waited on the ramp to drop.

IG led the way down, and the moment his tires hit the pavement, he took off like a bullet into the morning sunlight. I followed his lead, pushing my bike up to 120 mph with ease while managing not to cum from the dual sensations of the engine's power and Gini's pussy.

"This is f-fucking amazing Leroy," she said breathlessly.

"Just hang on," I instructed.

Traffic was flowing at a fast pace which definitely made things easier, but the scary part was the slight movements I was making to coincide with her hips lifting to take the dick. One wrong move at this speed and we'd be nothing more than a blurred line on the highway. The crazy part was that me knowing this only turned me on more and made my dick harder!

"Rush hour traffic ahead! Take the shoulder," IG said, coming across three lanes with ease.

"Ahhhhh shit L!" Gini moaned, signaling the arrival of her next climax wave.

I couldn't stop anything at the moment, so I popped the clutch and swerved behind IG while Gini surrendered herself to me. The way her pussy was throbbing, and twitching had my dick jumping like it came with a bungee cord, and before I knew it, I was cumming with her. I didn't realize that I'd opened the throttle up when I was momentarily distracted, but my bike suddenly started shaking and the speedometer read 201 mph.

I tapped the back breaks and that threw me into Gini, which set orgasmic lights off in my head that had me lost in her magic again. The moment I saw the light bar for the state trooper ahead of me though, I snapped out of it and applied more pressure to the brakes. The squealing sounds of my tires protesting echoed loudly through the morning air accompanied by the sickening smell of rubber, metal and plastic.

I ignored all of that though and focused on maintaining control of the bike because it was getting loose fast.

"Hold on tight," I demanded. Swerving back into traffic and riding the centerline.

I blew past the cop car close enough to see the steam wafting up from the mug he had at his hips, but I didn't dare worry about that or slowing down again; my mind was trapped in survival mode, while my dick wanted nothing more than to keep diving inside of her heavenly oasis.

"L, get back on the shoulder before that cop catches your tags," IG said.

As soon as I saw an opening in the traffic, I broke right, angling for the shoulder of the highway again. When I got there, I thought we were good, but then the shooting started.

Aryanna

Chapter 16
2028

Cyn's face was an open mask of truth that expressed pain and fear in equal measure, which served as the final straw in convincing me that she'd had her hands in me being shot. My own daughter had become my OPP and tried to erase me from the earth.

"Bae, did you hear me? I said your stepdad Steven is dead," Rome repeated, crossing the room to where Cyn was.

"I heard you," Cyn replied softly, staring off into space.

"Damn sis, I'm sorry, I know that you loved him like a real dad," Lia said.

"She loved him more than her real dad...which is why she helped him try to kill me this morning," I stated calmly, looking at Cyn to gauge her reaction.

My words made everybody freeze, but all eyes still swung from me to Cyn and back to me.

"Your stepdad is the cop that went after our father?" Lia asked, with obvious disbelief in her voice.

Cyn didn't reply, but the look of guilt she wore transformed her face into that of a little girl who knew she was gonna get her ass whipped for what she'd done.

"You can't prove that Cyn had anything to do with whatever happened to you," Rome said, taking a protective step towards Cyn.

"Prove? The look on her fucking face is proof enough!" Lia yelled.

Rome was too busy engaging with Lia to pay me any attention, which gave me the split second that I needed to pull the Hellcat out of my pocket. There was no movie-style theatrics, I simply upped the pistol and shot Rome between his eyes. The shock from everyone was like standing still, despite everyone's ability to move around. By the time the lil nigga hit the ground, I had the gun trained on Cyn and my conscience was firmly in check.

"Dad wait," Lia said, quickly rising and moving in front of her sister.

"Move Lia, this don't got shit to do with you," I said calmly.

"It does have something to do with me because you're my dad and Cyn is my sister. You can't shoot her Pops, even if she deserves the harshest lessons that life can offer her. At the end of the day, she's still your daughter!"

The look of pleading in Lia's eyes was touching and it was pulling at all the humanity I had in me, but it wasn't as simple as letting Cyn live. Cyn was a snake, so my survival instincts told me that getting rid of her now was the only way to prevent getting bit again. The decision I wanted to make was warring with the decision the father in me knew that I was supposed to make, which gave me pause.

I expected to see fear when I looked into Cyn's eyes, but instead, I found the most unlikely of things. Her eye's held humor.

"Something funny Cyn?" I asked.

"A lot of shit about this is funny, but mainly the idea that you would actually shoot your own daughter. You go hard Leroy, but not that hard," Cyn replied.

"Bitch shut up," Lia said, elbowing Cyn while keeping her eyes on me.

I felt the blood in my veins get slightly warmer, which caused me to smile at Cyn in a way that I knew didn't reach my eyes. It kinda amazed me that after the stories her mom had told her about me when she was growing up that she would still think I was incapable of taking her life. I'd helped in the creation of her life, which meant it was mine in a way.

This was the moment in time when she would know that lesson.

"Cyn, I think you have the wrong impression of me and what I'm capable of. I also know that you're too young to have mastered this saying, but I want you to listen to me closely: **When you take a shot at the King...don't miss**," I said.

"The King? Who's King are you supposed to be Leroy?! You're a half ass criminal who is a part-time father that still doesn't amount to shit! You'll NEVER be a King...but my mom was a Queen, even though you tried your damnedest to take that from her. She means more to me dead than you ever will alive! So, don't ever consider yourself my King or anybody's King because you're not worthy of a crown," Cyn replied, passionately.

"I can tell that you've always blamed me for the things that have gone wrong in your life, while you've put your mom on a pedestal as a Queen. Your reality is disturbed baby girl, but nothing I can say will get you to see that or change your view, so I won't waste either of our time. Just answer this question for me, did you know that Lt. Steven Hogan was gonna try to kill me?"

The smirk on her face transformed into a full-fledged smile that was as beautiful as the ones she'd graced me with when she was my little Daddy's Girl. Seeing it now froze my heart in my chest.

"Of course, I knew he was gonna try to kill you. Steve was my real dad in every way that'll ever matter, and we had no secrets between us. He knew that I wanted you to die for what you did to my mom, and he felt the same way. My only regret is that you're standing there instead of him but trust me dear old dad, you'll get what's coming to you sooner than later," Cyn replied.

"So will you sweetheart," I said, adjusting my aim so that her brown left eye could see clearly down the gun's barrel.

"Pops don't-."

Lia never got the chance to finish her plea before I swiftly tapped the trigger, and instantly reunited Cyn with her mom and stepdad. Lia flinched and scrambled away from the sound of her sister's body collapsing on top of her boyfriend.

"Oh-Oh my God Dad. She-She was pregnant," Lia cried out, scurrying from the room.

A few seconds later, I heard the sounds of violent vomiting and crying. I sincerely wanted to go comfort my remaining daughter, but in reality, what the fuck could I say to her that could justify what I'd done? There were no words invented by God that could explain away the fact that I'd just blown my daughter's brains out, and as a byproduct, I'd murdered my grandchild too. As the seconds passed, I could feel the numbness taking over more and more of me, until my emotions were buried in a bunker deep enough to be beside the earth's crust.

When I looked down at the gun in my hand, my brain shifted gears and the survival instinct kicked in. the sounds of Lia still throwing up could be heard clearly, and for a second, I actually considered her a threat as a witness, but I quickly banished those thoughts. I tucked my pistol, pulled out my burner phone and texted IG.

I couldn't explain what the hell had just transpired, even if it wasn't crazy as fuck to put that info out over open airwaves, so I just sent him my current location and told him to get here right-the-fuck-now. With that done, I repeated the procedures that were becoming routine when it comes to setting the stage for whoever would see this scene. I gathered up all traces of me, including everything Lia had used to sew me up and I stuffed it into my bag,

I shot Lewy a text and gave him my location so that he could disable cameras and erase everything in a 5-mile radius from the past 48 hours. I had to make it look like this situation and scene were part of what had taken place at my spot not long ago, and that way, I could see the theory of me being targeted. Doing it this way would also buy me time and allow me to disappear because anyone being hunted would go underground.

As I was standing in front of Cyn and Rome's bodies, debating about whether or not to wipe the gun and leave it, Lia came back into the room holding a washcloth up to her mouth. When our eyes locked, I saw her pain and confusion, which were accepted, but I also saw her fear and the way her eyes flickered to the gun in my hand.

"I'll never hurt you, Lia. I know that may be hard for you to believe right now, and I don't have time to convince you, but if you don't believe me then shoot me," I said turning the gun around so that the handle was extended towards her.

She looked at it for a few seconds before meeting my steady gaze again and shaking her head.

"Wh-What happens now?" she asked softly.

No sooner has the question left her mouth than my phone vibrated in my other hand from an incoming text. I felt slight relief from the words I read, even though I knew this was only the beginning.

"One of my men just pulled up and we're gonna figure it out from there. What I need you to do is get your phone because when I tell you to, I want you to call 911," I replied.

"Wait, you want me to call the cops?"

Her disbelief cut through her confusion quickly, and I was glad that she was alert versus teetering on the edge of shock.

"Yeah, I'ma have you call the cops, but we gotta get the story straight. First of all, I was never here today, and I've already cleaned up the shit you used to dew me up. I'm not trying to have to burn your spot down, so if they dust for prints and find mine then just tell them I came over to give you some money. You don't know where I went or where I was coming from, I just dropped some cash on you and left. If they ask you when I was here just say yesterday. But I didn't stay long.

When they question you about them getting shot, I want you to say that you woke up when you heard gunshots, and you didn't come out of your room immediately because you didn't know if people were in the house. This will explain why it took some time for you to call 911. They'll ask you the typical questions about your enemies because this is your house, and they'll ask about your relationship with Cyn.

I know that you can handle all of that without me coaching you, so I'm not gonna waste time on that. Just keep shit simple, and all of this will be behind you before you know it," I reassured her.

"No, it won't Pops."

I didn't argue with her simply because I could see the pain clouding her eyes, and I knew it would be fucked up to minimize the fact that she'd lost someone she loved.

"I'll be right back," I said, going to the front door.

When I pulled the door open, Zuk was standing there, wearing his own look of confusion. I mouthed for him to follow me as I led the way back inside the apartment. When we came to the bodies, Zuk looked at me for an explanation, but since I hadn't rehearsed exactly what I was gonna say I just gave him the story I'd outlined for Lia.

"Sounds like you've got everything under control, so why did you need me to come out here?" he asked.

"Because two heads are better than one, and three are better than two, so I wanted to make sure that in my heightened state of agitation, I ain't missing something that'll get me fucked later-," I replied truthfully.

"Makes sense, I don't see anything that you missed, and I definitely don't wanna contaminate the scene with my DNA, so I'ma get up out of here. Actually, you should be coming with me so that your daughter can get the ball rolling," he said.

I knew that he was right, but I was hesitant to leave my daughter here for a few different reasons. I'd never question her strength because she'd been baptized by fire her entire life, and she was definitely that diamond in the rough. This situation was a different test, a different experience than she'd ever had to face before, and I couldn't predict how she would handle it.

"I'll meet you outside Zuk, just let me holla at my lil one really quick."

He nodded in understanding and left us alone. I didn't really know how to begin to say what I needed to say, so I bought time by putting my backpack back on and looking around for anything that was mine. When that was done, I stood in front of her so that I could face the music.

"Lia, listen, I-."

"I don't wanna hear it dad. Whatever you're about to say won't fix this or make it any better, so just don't," she said forcefully.

"I know I can't undo this, but if you'll let me explain-."

"You can't explain this shit to me like I wasn't right there to witness it from the jump! You can't spin the situation, and you damn sure can't spin me, so just stop! I'll do what you asked, and I'll say whatever I gotta say, but after that, I'm done. We're done," she stated.

The look in her eyes was unnerving and more than determined, which made my heart drop.

"What are you saying Lia?"

"I'm saying you lost two daughters today because I want nothing to do with you."

Chapter 17
2027

All I could spare was a glance in my side mirror at these speeds, but that was enough for me to see the state police officer taking aim to fire another shot in my direction.

"IG, he's shooting at me!" I said, twisting the throttle harder to demand more speed from my bike.

"Just keep moving and stay right behind me," IG replied.

"B-Baby?" Gini said, squeezing her legs to get my attention.

For a moment, I'd forgotten that she was beneath me with my dick still oozing cum inside her tight hot pussy.

"It's ok babe, just hang on," I replied, focusing on the road ahead.

The sudden sounds of sirens had me checking my side mirror for the cops, but I didn't see anyone. There were only a few Rulers behind me at this point, which meant the others must've been holding the law that was on our asses. I kept my eyes forward as the power harnessed as my street beast continued to eat up the road with the force and determination of angry termites.

A short 10 minutes later, I saw signs welcoming me into the commonwealth of Kentucky. I followed IG closely until we pulled into another rest stop a few miles inside the state line, and then the baton was passed.

"Baby you need to switch positions," I said, coming to a stop beside our new 20 bike motorcade.

Her pussy was so tight that I literally had to pull us apart so that she could climb off my bike and climb on behind me.

I made sure to put my dick away before signaling that we were ready to go.

"Switch to channel 2L, you'll be talking to Dana, she leads the Rulers out here. She'll take care of you," IG said.

"Aightbruh. I appreciate you for everything. I meant that."

"Thought is the Ruler," IG said.

"And Ruler is supreme," I replied.

Once IG pulled off, I switched over the mic in my helmet to channel 2.

"Dana?"

"Peace King. We'll make sure you get through Kentucky safely. Follow us, but stay in the middle of the pack," she said.

"I gotcha," I replied.

She nodded once, and then eased off on her Ducati 916 that was painted custom purple with a black unicorn on the side of the gas tank.

"Babe, can you hear me?" I asked.

"I'm with you L," Gini replied wrapping herself around me from behind me and laying her helmet against my back.

I pulled off and merged in with Dana's crew slowly, but once we were back on the interstate, we were hauling ass again. There was less traffic which allowed us to set the flow at 120 mph easily. Even at those speeds though, it still took us an hour to reach the destination of a huge house that sat on at least 10 acres of cleared land converted into one hell of a weed growing operation.

"Damn Dana, is all of this yours?" I asked, impressed by the rows of marijuana plants that stretched as far as the eyes could see.

"No, not all mine. Ours! This farm is property of Ruler nation, and it was founded using the money that you, Zuk and IG made off of distributing future. IG didn't want us dealing with hard drugs out here, but weed is a legal Billion-dollar industry, and we've got our hands in the pie," she stated proudly.

"I see," I said bringing my bike to a stop in front of the house.

I had no idea how many bedrooms were in this spot, but it looked big enough to comfortably house everyone in the crew and then some. Once Gini hopped off, I followed her lead while pulling my helmet off. When I turned to Gini, she had the helmet in her hands, and the most beautiful grin stretching across her face as she stared off into the distance.

"So, this is freedom, huh?" she asked.

"Yeah baby, and you're never going back," I vowed.

"Do you promise Leroy? I don't need you to promise me the world and all the things in it, I just need you to promise to keep me safe and free."

"I swear on my life," I said, putting my helmet down and pulling her into my arms.

I kissed her soft lips tenderly, yet passionately, and held her tight enough to allow her to catch life from my beating heart. When I pulled back and looked down into her eyes, I saw her complete trust staring back at me, and it was a beautiful sight.

"I'm sure that you will wanna get some food and some rest given your recent exploits, so follow me," Dana said.

I recognized her voice from when I'd had my helmet on, but it hadn't prepared me for the sight of her. I'd expected a cute white girl but standing in her place was a gorgeous caramel complexion black woman with the curves one might find on a mountain road. If the helmet she was cradling didn't match her bike I would've simply mistaken her for

141

one of the other members, but there was no mistaking the 5'2, 150lbs with the hazel eyes for anybody else.

Especially not with the purple dreadlocks she had now spilling about her shoulders.

"You're beautiful," Gini blurted, causing Dana to blush slightly.

"Thank you, so are you."

When I looked back at the woman in my arms, I could see the twinkle in her eyes, and I knew that she was imagining some type of sexual scenario in her mind.

"Do you like girls Dana?" Gini asked.

My laughter was instant and uncontrollable because her question only confirmed my suspicions.

"No, I don't like girls. I do however love women though," Dana replied.

My laughter got stuck in my throat as my eyes swung back to Dana, and I found the same twinkle of enchantment in her eyes. There was no doubt in my mind that trouble was coming.

"Follow me, and I'll show you to your room," Dana said, chuckling softly.

Without a word, Gini grabbed my hand and fell in step behind Dana. I knew that both of us had our eyes locked on the way Dana's hips swayed, and how that resulted in her juicy booty jiggling as she walked.

Her ass wasn't on the same wavelength as Gini's, but it was definitely noteworthy enough to have me envisioning what it would feel like bouncing off my thighs while I ran dick through her. We followed her inside the plantation-style mansion that had no doubt housed slave masters and upstairs to the second floor. We were led down the hallway until about the midway point, and then, we stepped inside a room on the left side.

The house was old, but it had been severely upgraded so that it was modern in every way which made it comfortable. The sleigh bed looked as soft as the fluffy pillows that were piled around the headboard, and I could barely see the wall behind the huge 80" flat screen covering it. The floor was mahogany brown wood that looked heated under the bright lights of the hanging crystal chandelier.

"The bathroom is through that door to your right, and your private balcony is through the double doors straight ahead," Dana said, pointing.

"How private is the balcony?" Gini asked.

Dana stopped and turned to look at her with a devilish smile on her face.

"Well, we can hear you if you scream loud enough, but we won't see what's making you feel so good," she replied.

"Do you wanna see?" Gini asked, smiling right back at her.

Dana's eyes flickered towards me quickly before coming back to meet my wife's steady gaze.

"Do I get 2 for one?" Dana asked.

"Of course," Gini said.

"Interesting," Dana replied, licking her lips.

"I should warn you that my wife and I have larger appetites when it comes to sex," I said.

"Oh, I'm sure you do…but it won't hurt to find out when and if the time comes. For now, why don't you two relax and decompress, while I get everything prepared for the next leg of your journey? You're not due to leave for 2 days, but if the heat somehow gets too hot, it'll be good to have the continuing plans in place," Dana said.

"Agreed," Gini replied.

They shared a long look before Dana finally left the room, which told me all I needed to know.

A 3-some on your first day out bae?" I asked, chuckling and shaking my head.

"Go ahead and act like you got a problem with it when I know how you've been living your life. I wanna have some fun with you too."

I took her in my arms and just held her close for a moment, relishing the fact that there was no Correctional Officer to tell us to separate.

"I love you Gingerbread."

"And I love you, my husband. I love you so fucking much!"

As badly as I wanted to rip her clothes off and have her climbing every wall in this room for starters, I simply held her and lived in the moment. The days and nights that we'd spent together and apart imagining this exact moment in time were pointless, but they were all with it. That hope of one day doing exactly what we were doing now had motivated us to pull off the unthinkable, and it had cemented our love in a way that no one who hadn't lived our lives could imagine.

"I-I can't believe you did it L. I mean, you really put it all on the line for me, and gave up everything in the process."

"I've got everything I need right here baby," I said softly, hugging her to me tighter.

I could feel the trembling in her body, and I knew the day's adrenaline had finally worn off enough for her to have a good cry. I didn't judge her, nor did I say anything, I just held my wife and gave her the love that she deserved.

"Uh, I hate to interrupt, but you two need to see this," Dana said, coming back into the room and moving to the TV.

Gini took a step back so that she could turn towards the TV, but I quickly felt her fingers interlock with my own. The first image we saw when Dana brought the screen to life was Gini's mugshot, right beside her co-defendant, Pony.

"...Sylvia Brooks has the latest on this strange and twisted tale. Sylvia?"

"Thanks Ron. I'm here at the Wallens Ridge state prison in Big Stone Gap, Virginia where a man named Pony McDaniels was found dead by suicide in his cell a few hours ago. Sadly, suicide isn't an uncommon thing in prison, but what separates this particular case from the norm is the note that Pony left behind. It was serving, as well as his continued criminal activities up to the moment of his suicide. The note said in part,

'Since I'm a snitch anyway, let me go ahead and tell it all. The attack on fluvanna was orchestrated by me because Virginia Bly had to die. It doesn't matter how many people die with her as long as I got that bitch!'

Now Ron, as you know there were mass casualties in that attack on Fluvanna Women's prison and I've already confirmed that Virginia Bly was Pony McDanielsco-defendant, and she was in fact killed early this morning. So, it would seem that we now have an explanation behind those horrific events...or do we? A source inside the Fairfax Police Department had confirmed that an anonymous call was traced back to a woman calling herself Candice Bly and that in this call, Candice offers up a different story altogether. Candice insists that the attack on Fluvanna Correctional Center wasn't so much an attack as it was a diversion for what would be the most daring prison break in modern history. What lends credence to this alternative theory is that Virginia Bly's husband, Leroy Bly, has mysteriously vanished. Leroy Bly is a successful entrepreneur who owns a string of businesses, but his tired to ties to the street and organized crime are as prolific as his business acumen.

At this time, Mr. Bly is only wanted for questioning, but we'll keep you posted on all of this growing chaos as it unfolds. I'm Sylvia Burns, NBC News..."

I could feel the sweat pouring from Gini's palm like her fingers had suddenly learned how to cry, but I dared not let her hand up. Right now, we were the only thing keeping each other standing.

"How do you wanna play this L," Dana asked.

"C-Candi sold us out," Gini said, in disbelief.

"Hell hath no fury like a woman scorned," I said softly.

"But-But-But I let her be with you! I let both of them bitches play house with you!" Gini raged.

"It sounds like somebody wanted more than just a slice of the pie, and if she can't have it, then nobody can," Dana said.

The truth in her words only made me angrier, but I knew that anger wouldn't get me out of this situation. It was gonna take cool, calculated thought and a lot of muthafuckin patience.

"It's only a matter of time before the Feds start liking theory number 2 and running with it, which means we need to iron out this escape plan until it's perfect. Call a meeting for all Supreme Rulers Dana because it gonna take every connection we've got to get us out of this alive. I've come too far to die now."

Chapter 18
2022
(One month later)

"What's wrong Leroy, you didn't seem too happy to see me? Am I not what you expected?"

"It's not that Gini, my mind is just all over the place."

She took my hand in her, forcing me to look her in the eyes and expose my inner pain. I'd felt like my life had been doing nothing but spiraling out of control ever since I got out of prison. There had been good things to happen as far as the business opportunities that came my way, but the black clouds of death and destruction had a way of blocking any amount of sunlight. Gini had been the only light that I could still see, and I was beyond grateful for that.

"Your ass is crazy, and you know that right?" she asked, smiling that beautiful, crooked smile I'd come to love.

"Why do you say that?"

"How else do you describe a man who marries a chick he just met in order to be able to visit her, L?"

"A man in love," I replied simply.

The way she looked at me with her heart in her eyes made my palms sweat and my heart beat faster with each passing second. When she leaned towards me over the small table separating us, I immediately mirrored her movements until our lips came together. Our first kiss was an innocent peck of exploration, but that quickly morphed into a three-alarm blaze of fire that had my ears ringing and my feet tapping by the time I pulled back.

"Wow," I murmured, looking deep into the blue of her eyes.

"Right back at you. I've never been kissed like that."

"Well, I can promise you more of the same if you want," I replied, smiling at her.

"Oh, I know you can, and you'll deliver on that promise too, my Husband. I just wish I could experience all you have to offer in the bedroom,"

"You will, I promise," I said.

The smile on her face froze and the light in her eyes dimmed a little bit. For a moment, her beauty was locked in a time capsule, and I felt like I couldn't reach her. Before I was controlled by panic though, the moment was gone, and she'd returned to being right here with me.

"If you say so L, but I doubt either of us will live another 1200 years for me to complete this sentence."

"Who says that we have to, baby? Do you really think I'm gonna let my wife die in this place?" I asked.

"How are you gonna get me out, L?"

I looked around to make sure that I wasn't being over-heard before I leaned towards her and motioned for her to move closer. I whispered to her for a couple of minutes before sitting back in my seat and watching her closely. The kaleidoscope of emotions that contorted her features only enhanced her beauty, and it made me smile.

"Your ass is really crazy," she said, laughing joyfully.

"Of course, I am, but it's my most enduring quality."

"Tell me about the other qualities that I now get to reap the benefits of," she said, crossing her legs sensually and sitting back to give me her undivided attention.

We spent the next two hours getting to know each other in a way that our constant phone calls didn't capture. The time flew so fast that we were both startled when the Correctional Officer approached us and announced that our time was up. Both of us wanted to give his ass directions to hell, but we wanna fuck our future plans up so I left quietly, after kissing her like we were fighting for oxygen.

Once I was back behind the wheel of my truck, I sat there for a moment and contemplated my next move for the day. I honestly wanted nothing more than to be spending my day making sweet love to my wife, but since that wasn't possible, I had to find an alternative. When my phone vibrated, I grabbed it out of the center console and checked my text messages.

Tonio was a nigga I'd done time with that I'd kept in touch with, but I didn't feel like fucking with him today. His text did give me an idea though, and my fingers immediately started flying across the screen. Within two minutes, a text came back that made me point my truck in the direction of Alexandria, VA. An hour and a half later, I was knocking on Candice's apartment door. She opened the door wearing only a t-shirt and some socks with her nipples poking out like quarters through the thin cotton.

"Does Tonio know you're here?"

"Not unless you told him," I replied, pushing her gently back into the apartment.

"I'm not telling him shit that ain't his business, and this definitely ain't his business."

"I agree, so what's up? When I was locked up you talked big shit about how good that pussy is, and how it's too wet for me to stay in. You gonna back that big mouth up?" I asked, unzipping my pants and pulling my dick out.

She looked down and licked her lips before slowly getting on her knees.

"Don't cum in my mouth, I want you to save that for this good pussy."

I wrapped my left hand up in her hair while grabbing my dick with my right and guided the two together until we connected like legos. That was the beginning of what turned into a long afternoon and a long night. The pussy was as good as advertised, but the dick was better, and I delivered with a mission in mind. By the time the sun rose the following morning, I had her bring me breakfast and feed me while I relaxed against her headboard.

"So, what made you finally come see me? Not that I'm complaining," she said quickly.

"I don't know...I was sexually frustrated, and I needed some pussy that I'd never had before."

"You were more than sexually frustrated bae because you got my pussy sore as shit," she replied, laughing while guiding a fork full of eggs to my mouth.

I chewed thoughtfully and reflected on what I'd done to Candice, even though I knew that I'd been thinking about Gini the entire time. They were polar opposite in looks, but it didn't matter because it was still new pussy, so I could imagine more vividly that it was my wife I was fucking. Undoubtedly, Gini would be way better at playing mattress tag with me, but Candice would do for now.

"What's wrong sweetheart, you can't take the pounding?" I asked, smirking.

"Oh, I can take it boo, and if I can't, I got somebody to help carry the load."

"Oh really?" I asked, intrigued.

"Yeap. You remember my homegirl Amelia, right?"

"Vaguely, but what about her?" I asked.

"She's down for whatever, and she has no limitations....so, if you want me to, I'll bring her into whatever this is between us."

I didn't respond immediately, but I gave her offer enough thought to refuse the next bite of food that she tried to push my way; I was good at math, so I knew that getting two for the price of one was always a steal. At the same time, having that many women meant twice the problems and double the personality management, which meant extreme caution was necessary.

"Let me think about that Candice."

"Really? What's there to think about L? You're getting the royal treatment, and all you have to do is come home to get it," she said.

"Did you factor my wife into all this?"

"I didn't know you had a wife," she replied, surprised.

"Well, I do, and I love her."

Candice absorbed the hit of this information like a bullet between the eyes, but her recovery time reminded me of a zombie.

"Tell me about her," she said.

"Are you serious right now?"

"I'm dead serious Leroy, now tell me about your wife."

I took a few seconds to choose my words carefully before I began speaking. Before I could really speak to Gini's character and what had made me fall in love with her, I heard the sound of a door opening and closing.

"Did you hear that?" I asked.

The panic-stricken look on Candice's face said it all and that made me quickly scramble out of the bed.

"I left my gun in my truck," I whispered.

She hurriedly put the plate of food aside and made a mad dash for her bedroom closet. I heard her going through some boxes and then she returned a few moments later with something purple clutched in her grip.

"What the hell is that?" I asked.

"It's a Ruger .25, custom painted my favorite color. It shoots accurate and that's all that matters," she replied, passing it to me.

I took it, dropped the clip to make sure it was fully loaded, slammed the clip back in and chambered a round. Me finishing my inspection coincided with the doorknob on the bedroom turning. I upped the pistol and prepared for shit to go really badly really quick.

"Hey ma, you sleep?"

"Oh my God, it's just Tonio," Candice said with obvious relief in her tone.

I didn't share the same sentiments as her, though because I'd just been caught fucking my niggas momma.

"For real bruh?" Tonio asked, staring pointedly at me.

"Tonio, don't start, please. Go wait for me in the living room," Candice said.

I could tell by his laser beams on me that he wasn't paying his mom any attention, which was why I had yet to lower the gun. I felt vulnerable because I was standing here naked and having the gun in my hand helped with that too.

"Didn't I tell you not to fuck my mother?" he asked, taking a step towards me.

"Don't do this bruh," I warned.

"Tonio!" Candice said forcefully.

"You have way too many women on your radar than to need pussy, so you fucked her just because, you bitch ass nigga," he said, taking another step closer.

"I'm telling you to chill my nigga because you don't know what's going on here," I replied calmly.

"Tonio, go wait in the living room," Candice demanded.

"Nah, fuck that, I'ma kill this nigga!" Tonio declared loudly, reaching behind his back.

My instincts told me to pull the trigger, but I ignored that and gave him the benefit of the doubt. As soon as I saw the gun in his hand I knew I could no longer do that though.

"Tonio, No!" Candice screamed.

Before she could move, he made the mistake of trying to raise the gun in my direction, and for that act of hostility, I tapped the trick letting a bullet change his mind. The lifeless look in his eyes somehow still held some anger, but he was beyond doing anything about it at this point. Complete silence followed the sound of his body hitting the floor and when I looked at Candice, I read the shock all over her face.

I didn't know what to do, so I simply sat down on the bed and tried to comprehend how everything had gone so wrong. This hadn't been my intention when I'd hit Candice up, and I damn sure hadn't planned on her son finding out like this. I couldn't unwind the clock though, and this was a bell only God could unring.

"You-You killed my son," she murmured in a dazed tone.

"I didn't want to sweetheart. I truly didn't want shit to end like this."

She didn't say anything as she slowly approached his body and stood over him. I had no idea what she was feeling at this moment, but I knew enough to keep the gun in my hand ready for scene two. I didn't know what she was doing when she bent down, but when I saw her pick up his gun I slipped my finger inside the trigger guard and rested it on the trigger.

"Candice please don't make this situation worse," I said.

She turned around slowly until she was facing me, but she kept the gun pressed against her thick thigh.

"It doesn't get worst Leroy."

I kept my eyes on hers so that I'd be able to see the moment when she didn't wanna live anymore.

"I didn't wanna shoot him Candice, honestly. If he hadn't tried to up his gun, I wouldn't have shot him."

"I believe you, but that's not gonna bring my son back. Which means you owe me," she said, moving slowly towards me.

"Owe you what?"

She stopped right in front of me and pushed me back on the bed while she climbed on top of me.

"I'll take this for starters," she said, squeezing my dick until it was hard enough for her to slide down on it.

"Canice wait we can't-."

"*shhhhh*! Don't talk because nothing you say will undo what you did. You owe me your life, so shut up and fuck me."

Chapter 19
2027

"The simplest solution is to eliminate Candice and that means taking care of Amelia, but I doubt anyone knows where they are right now," I said, staring at the pensive looks from my constituents who were in the group conference on the laptop.

"Do they have family we can exploit?" IG asked.

"I mean yeah, but at this point, if the Feds have them in some back room making a deal, then nothing is gonna flush them out," I replied.

"We've got people inside every branch of law enforcement and all of them all want this story to die quickly," Zuk pointed out.

"That's a fact," Bamm stated.

"How much time do we have realistically though?" Dana asked.

"Every second counts, but we still have to move strategically," I said.

"Agreed," IG stated.

"Regardless of what story the law chooses to run with, it's still gonna be considered domestic terrorism and they're gonna want everybody involved to pay for that. Pony being the fall guy was only a temporary fix to all for the time to get you and Gini out of the country safely, but I think that's a moot point either way" Zuk stated.

"Dana, are they safe there?" IG asked.

"For now, yeah. The question is whether or not him being a Ruler is gonna show up in black and white because if that happens, then all safety measures are compromised," Dana replied.

"Despite the legality of our organization, I still move like I did in my former life as a gang member, which means there's no paper trail. I can't speak about whether or not there will be speculation or not," I said.

Everyone absorbed this information silently and I could see the wheels spinning behind the eyes staring at me from miles away. The unspoken question was whether or not I was a liability or an asset, and if I was labelled the former, would anyone actually try to get rid of me and Gini. I looked over the top of the laptop's monitor and locked eyes with my wife, who'd been sitting out of view in a chair in the corner of our room.

It was clear to see that she understood the unspoken conversation that was taking place, but there was no worry in her eyes.

"L. Do you think it's safe for you to proceed with the plan until you're out of the country?" IG asked.

The fact that he put this to me as a question told me that he wasn't trying to send me out into traffic, and I knew the loyalty was still intact.

"Nah, I think misdirection is our best weapon. Besides, it's my fault that we're under fire because I trusted the wrong bitch. It's my mess and I gotta clean it up. We're not running when there's still killing to do...."

To Be Continued...
Til Death 2
Coming Soon

Lock Down Publications and Ca$h Presents assisted publishing packages.

BASIC PACKAGE $499
Editing
Cover Design
Formatting

UPGRADED PACKAGE $800
Typing
Editing
Cover Design
Formatting

ADVANCE PACKAGE $1,200
Typing
Editing
Cover Design
Formatting
Copyright registration
Proofreading
Upload book to Amazon

LDP SUPREME PACKAGE $1,500
Typing
Editing
Cover Design
Formatting
Copyright registration
Proofreading
Set up Amazon account

Upload book to Amazon
Advertise on LDP Amazon and Facebook page

***Other services available upon request. Additional charges may apply
Lock Down Publications
P.O. Box 944
Stockbridge, GA 30281-9998
Phone # 470 303-9761

Submission Guideline

Submit the first three chapters of your completed manuscript to ldpsubmissions@gmail.com, subject line: Your book's title. The manuscript must be in a .doc file and sent as an attachment. Document should be in Times New Roman, double spaced and in size 12 font. Also, provide your synopsis and full contact information. If sending multiple submissions, they must each be in a separate email.

Have a story but no way to send it electronically? You can still submit to LDP/Ca$h Presents. Send in the first three chapters, written or typed, of your completed manuscript to:

LDP: Submissions Dept
Po Box 944
Stockbridge, Ga 30281

DO NOT send original manuscript. Must be a duplicate.

Provide your synopsis and a cover letter containing your full contact information.

Thanks for considering LDP and Ca$h Presents.

<u>NEW RELEASES</u>

PROTÉGÉ OF A LEGEND by COREY ROBINSON
STRAIGHT BEAST MODE 2 by DE'KARI
ANGEL 3 by ANTHONY FIELDS
CLASSIC CITY by CHRIS GREEN
TIL DEATH by ARYANNA

Til Death

<u>Coming Soon from Lock Down Publications/Ca$h Presents</u>

BLOOD OF A BOSS **VI**

SHADOWS OF THE GAME II

TRAP BASTARD II

By **Askari**

LOYAL TO THE GAME **IV**

By **T.J. & Jelissa**

TRUE SAVAGE **VIII**

MIDNIGHT CARTEL IV

DOPE BOY MAGIC IV

CITY OF KINGZ III

NIGHTMARE ON SILENT AVE II

THE PLUG OF LIL MEXICO II

CLASSIC CITY II

By **Chris Green**

BLAST FOR ME **III**

A SAVAGE DOPEBOY III

CUTTHROAT MAFIA III

DUFFLE BAG CARTEL VII

HEARTLESS GOON VI

By **Ghost**

A HUSTLER'S DECEIT III

KILL ZONE II

BAE BELONGS TO ME III

TIL DEATH II

By **Aryanna**

KING OF THE TRAP III

By **T.J. Edwards**
GORILLAZ IN THE BAY V
3X KRAZY III
STRAIGHT BEAST MODE III
De'Kari
KINGPIN KILLAZ IV
STREET KINGS III
PAID IN BLOOD III
CARTEL KILLAZ IV
DOPE GODS III
Hood Rich
SINS OF A HUSTLA II
ASAD
RICH $AVAGE II
By Martell Troublesome Bolden
YAYO V
Bred In The Game 2
S. Allen
CREAM III
THE STREETS WILL TALK II
By Yolanda Moore
SON OF A DOPE FIEND III
HEAVEN GOT A GHETTO II
By Renta
LOYALTY AIN'T PROMISED III
By Keith Williams
I'M NOTHING WITHOUT HIS LOVE II

SINS OF A THUG II

TO THE THUG I LOVED BEFORE II

IN A HUSTLER I TRUST II

By Monet Dragun

QUIET MONEY IV

EXTENDED CLIP III

THUG LIFE IV

By Trai'Quan

THE STREETS MADE ME IV

By **Larry D. Wright**

IF YOU CROSS ME ONCE II

ANGEL IV

By **Anthony Fields**

THE STREETS WILL NEVER CLOSE IV

By K'ajji

HARD AND RUTHLESS III

KILLA KOUNTY III

By Khufu

MONEY GAME III

By Smoove Dolla

JACK BOYS VS DOPE BOYS II

A GANGSTA'S QUR'AN V

COKE GIRLZ II

By Romell Tukes

MURDA WAS THE CASE II

Elijah R. Freeman

THE STREETS NEVER LET GO II

By Robert Baptiste

AN UNFORESEEN LOVE III

By **Meesha**

KING OF THE TRENCHES III
by **GHOST & TRANAY ADAMS**

MONEY MAFIA II

LOYAL TO THE SOIL III

By **Jibril Williams**

QUEEN OF THE ZOO II

By **Black Migo**

VICIOUS LOYALTY III

By Kingpen

A GANGSTA'S PAIN III

By J-Blunt

CONFESSIONS OF A JACKBOY III

By Nicholas Lock

GRIMEY WAYS II

By Ray Vinci

KING KILLA II

By Vincent "Vitto" Holloway

BETRAYAL OF A THUG II

By Fre$h

THE MURDER QUEENS II

By Michael Gallon

THE BIRTH OF A GANGSTER II

By Delmont Player

TREAL LOVE II

By Le'Monica Jackson

FOR THE LOVE OF BLOOD II

By Jamel Mitchell

RAN OFF ON DA PLUG II

By Paper Boi Rari

HOOD CONSIGLIERE II

By Keese

PRETTY GIRLS DO NASTY THINGS II

By Nicole Goosby

PROTÉGÉ OF A LEGEND II

By Corey Robinson

Available Now

RESTRAINING ORDER **I & II**

By **CA$H & Coffee**

LOVE KNOWS NO BOUNDARIES **I II & III**

By **Coffee**

RAISED AS A GOON I, II, III & IV

BRED BY THE SLUMS I, II, III

BLAST FOR ME I & II

ROTTEN TO THE CORE I II III

A BRONX TALE I, II, III

DUFFLE BAG CARTEL I II III IV V VI

HEARTLESS GOON I II III IV V

A SAVAGE DOPEBOY I II

DRUG LORDS I II III

CUTTHROAT MAFIA I II

KING OF THE TRENCHES

By **Ghost**

LAY IT DOWN **I & II**

LAST OF A DYING BREED I II

BLOOD STAINS OF A SHOTTA I & II III

By **Jamaica**

LOYAL TO THE GAME I II III

LIFE OF SIN I, II III

By **TJ & Jelissa**

BLOODY COMMAS I & II

SKI MASK CARTEL I II & III

KING OF NEW YORK I II,III IV V

RISE TO POWER I II III

COKE KINGS I II III IV V

BORN HEARTLESS I II III IV

KING OF THE TRAP I II

By **T.J. Edwards**

IF LOVING HIM IS WRONG…I & II

LOVE ME EVEN WHEN IT HURTS I II III

By **Jelissa**

WHEN THE STREETS CLAP BACK I & II III

THE HEART OF A SAVAGE I II III

MONEY MAFIA

LOYAL TO THE SOIL I II

By **Jibril Williams**

A DISTINGUISHED THUG STOLE MY HEART I II & III

LOVE SHOULDN'T HURT I II III IV

RENEGADE BOYS I II III IV

PAID IN KARMA I II III

SAVAGE STORMS I II III

AN UNFORESEEN LOVE I II

By **Meesha**

A GANGSTER'S CODE I &, II III

A GANGSTER'S SYN I II III

THE SAVAGE LIFE I II III

CHAINED TO THE STREETS I II III

BLOOD ON THE MONEY I II III

A GANGSTA'S PAIN I II

By J-Blunt

PUSH IT TO THE LIMIT

By **Bre' Hayes**

BLOOD OF A BOSS **I, II, III, IV, V**

SHADOWS OF THE GAME

TRAP BASTARD

By **Askari**

THE STREETS BLEED MURDER **I, II & III**

THE HEART OF A GANGSTA I II& III

By **Jerry Jackson**

CUM FOR ME I II III IV V VI VII VIII

An **LDP Erotica Collaboration**

BRIDE OF A HUSTLA **I II & II**

THE FETTI GIRLS **I, II& III**

CORRUPTED BY A GANGSTA I, II III, IV

BLINDED BY HIS LOVE

THE PRICE YOU PAY FOR LOVE I, II ,III

DOPE GIRL MAGIC I II III

By **Destiny Skai**

WHEN A GOOD GIRL GOES BAD

By **Adrienne**

THE COST OF LOYALTY I II III

By Kweli

A GANGSTER'S REVENGE **I II III & IV**

THE BOSS MAN'S DAUGHTERS I II III IV V

A SAVAGE LOVE **I & II**

BAE BELONGS TO ME I II

A HUSTLER'S DECEIT I, II, III

WHAT BAD BITCHES DO I, II, III

SOUL OF A MONSTER I II III

KILL ZONE

A DOPE BOY'S QUEEN I II III

TIL DEATH

By **Aryanna**

A KINGPIN'S AMBITON

A KINGPIN'S AMBITION **II**

I MURDER FOR THE DOUGH

By **Ambitious**

TRUE SAVAGE I II III IV V VI VII

DOPE BOY MAGIC I, II, III

MIDNIGHT CARTEL I II III

CITY OF KINGZ I II

NIGHTMARE ON SILENT AVE

THE PLUG OF LIL MEXICO II

CLASSIC CITY

By **Chris Green**

A DOPEBOY'S PRAYER

By **Eddie "Wolf" Lee**

THE KING CARTEL **I, II & III**

By **Frank Gresham**

THESE NIGGAS AIN'T LOYAL **I, II & III**

By **Nikki Tee**

GANGSTA SHYT **I II &III**

By **CATO**

THE ULTIMATE BETRAYAL

By **Phoenix**

BOSS'N UP **I , II & III**

By **Royal Nicole**

I LOVE YOU TO DEATH

By **Destiny J**

I RIDE FOR MY HITTA

I STILL RIDE FOR MY HITTA

By **Misty Holt**

LOVE & CHASIN' PAPER

By **Qay Crockett**

TO DIE IN VAIN

SINS OF A HUSTLA

By **ASAD**

BROOKLYN HUSTLAZ

By **Boogsy Morina**

BROOKLYN ON LOCK I & II

By **Sonovia**

GANGSTA CITY

By **Teddy Duke**

A DRUG KING AND HIS DIAMOND I & II III

A DOPEMAN'S RICHES

HER MAN, MINE'S TOO I, II

CASH MONEY HO'S

THE WIFEY I USED TO BE I II

PRETTY GIRLS DO NASTY THINGS

By Nicole Goosby

TRAPHOUSE KING **I II & III**

KINGPIN KILLAZ I II III

STREET KINGS I II

PAID IN BLOOD **I II**

CARTEL KILLAZ I II III

DOPE GODS I II

By **Hood Rich**

LIPSTICK KILLAH **I, II, III**

CRIME OF PASSION I II & III

FRIEND OR FOE I II III

By **Mimi**

STEADY MOBBN' **I, II, III**

THE STREETS STAINED MY SOUL I II III

By **Marcellus Allen**

WHO SHOT YA **I, II, III**

SON OF A DOPE FIEND I II

HEAVEN GOT A GHETTO

Renta

GORILLAZ IN THE BAY **I II III IV**

TEARS OF A GANGSTA I II

3X KRAZY I II

STRAIGHT BEAST MODE I II

DE'KARI

TRIGGADALE I II III

MURDARCBER WAS THE CASE

Elijah R. Freeman

GOD BLESS THE TRAPPERS I, II, III

THESE SCANDALOUS STREETS I, II, III

FEAR MY GANGSTA I, II, III IV, V

THESE STREETS DON'T LOVE NOBODY I, II

BURY ME A G I, II, III, IV, V

A GANGSTA'S EMPIRE I, II, III, IV

THE DOPEMAN'S BODYGAURD I II

THE REALEST KILLAZ I II III

THE LAST OF THE OGS I II III

Tranay Adams
THE STREETS ARE CALLING
Duquie Wilson
MARRIED TO A BOSS I II III
By Destiny Skai & Chris Green
KINGZ OF THE GAME I II III IV V VI
Playa Ray
SLAUGHTER GANG I II III
RUTHLESS HEART I II III
By Willie Slaughter
FUK SHYT
By Blakk Diamond
DON'T F#CK WITH MY HEART I II
By Linnea
ADDICTED TO THE DRAMA I II III
IN THE ARM OF HIS BOSS II
By Jamila
YAYO I II III IV
A SHOOTER'S AMBITION I II
BRED IN THE GAME
By S. Allen
TRAP GOD I II III
RICH $AVAGE
MONEY IN THE GRAVE I II III
By Martell Troublesome Bolden
FOREVER GANGSTA
GLOCKS ON SATIN SHEETS I II

By Adrian Dulan

TOE TAGZ I II III IV

LEVELS TO THIS SHYT I II

By Ah'Million

KINGPIN DREAMS I II III

RAN OFF ON DA PLUG

By Paper Boi Rari

CONFESSIONS OF A GANGSTA I II III IV

CONFESSIONS OF A JACKBOY I II

By Nicholas Lock

I'M NOTHING WITHOUT HIS LOVE

SINS OF A THUG

TO THE THUG I LOVED BEFORE

A GANGSTA SAVED XMAS

IN A HUSTLER I TRUST

By Monet Dragun

CAUGHT UP IN THE LIFE I II III

THE STREETS NEVER LET GO

By Robert Baptiste

NEW TO THE GAME I II III

MONEY, MURDER & MEMORIES I II III

By **Malik D. Rice**

LIFE OF A SAVAGE I II III

A GANGSTA'S QUR'AN I II III IV

MURDA SEASON I II III

GANGLAND CARTEL I II III

CHI'RAQ GANGSTAS I II III

KILLERS ON ELM STREET I II III

JACK BOYZ N DA BRONX I II III

A DOPEBOY'S DREAM I II III

JACK BOYS VS DOPE BOYS

COKE GIRLZ

By Romell Tukes

LOYALTY AIN'T PROMISED I II

By Keith Williams

QUIET MONEY I II III

THUG LIFE I II III

EXTENDED CLIP I II

By **Trai'Quan**

THE STREETS MADE ME I II III

By **Larry D. Wright**

THE ULTIMATE SACRIFICE I, II, III, IV, V, VI

KHADIFI

IF YOU CROSS ME ONCE

ANGEL I II III

IN THE BLINK OF AN EYE

By **Anthony Fields**

THE LIFE OF A HOOD STAR

By Ca$h & Rashia Wilson

THE STREETS WILL NEVER CLOSE I II III

By K'ajji

CREAM I II

THE STREETS WILL TALK

By Yolanda Moore

NIGHTMARES OF A HUSTLA I II III

By King Dream

CONCRETE KILLA I II III

VICIOUS LOYALTY I II

By Kingpen

HARD AND RUTHLESS I II

MOB TOWN 251

THE BILLIONAIRE BENTLEYS I II III

By Von Diesel

GHOST MOB

Stilloan Robinson

MOB TIES I II III IV V VI

By SayNoMore

BODYMORE MURDERLAND I II III

THE BIRTH OF A GANGSTER

By Delmont Player

FOR THE LOVE OF A BOSS

By C. D. Blue

MOBBED UP I II III IV

THE BRICK MAN I II III IV

THE COCAINE PRINCESS I II III IV V

By King Rio

KILLA KOUNTY I II III

By Khufu

MONEY GAME I II

By Smoove Dolla

A GANGSTA'S KARMA I II

By FLAME

KING OF THE TRENCHES I II

by **GHOST & TRANAY ADAMS**

QUEEN OF THE ZOO

By **Black Migo**

GRIMEY WAYS

By Ray Vinci

XMAS WITH AN ATL SHOOTER

By Ca$h & Destiny Skai

KING KILLA

By Vincent "Vitto" Holloway

BETRAYAL OF A THUG

By Fre$h

THE MURDER QUEENS

By Michael Gallon

TREAL LOVE

By Le'Monica Jackson

FOR THE LOVE OF BLOOD

By Jamel Mitchell

HOOD CONSIGLIERE

By Keese

PROTÉGÉ OF A LEGEND

By Corey Robinson

BOOKS BY LDP'S CEO, CA$H

TRUST IN NO MAN

TRUST IN NO MAN 2

TRUST IN NO MAN 3

BONDED BY BLOOD

SHORTY GOT A THUG

THUGS CRY

THUGS CRY 2

THUGS CRY 3

TRUST NO BITCH

TRUST NO BITCH 2

TRUST NO BITCH 3

TIL MY CASKET DROPS

RESTRAINING ORDER

RESTRAINING ORDER 2

IN LOVE WITH A CONVICT

LIFE OF A HOOD STAR

XMAS WITH AN ATL SHOOTER

Aryanna

www.ingramcontent.com/pod-product-compliance
Lightning Source LLC
Chambersburg PA
CBHW070526260626
47161CB00004B/1646